BLADE'S EDGE

L.A.S.T. DEFENSE

PATRICIA D. EDDY

For my baby girl, Abbie. You were my heart. My soul cat. My constant companion. My biggest cheerleader. All you ever wanted was love, and you gave it back a hundred-fold.
I've never written a book without you. Saying goodbye to you was the hardest thing I've ever done. I'll see you again one day, baby. Until then, I'll hold your memory close. Thank you for choosing me to be your mama. I love you.

If you love steamy romantic suspense, I'd love to send you an exclusive short story set in Dublin, Ireland. Castles & Kings is ONLY available for my newsletter subscribers. Visit my website and let me know where to send your free short story!
http://patriciadeddy.com

PROLOGUE

Eight Months Ago

Jasper

THE SCENT of stale coffee is about to do me in. That and Schaffer's constant crunching. Who the fuck brings Cheetos on a stakeout? I'm gonna need to get my car detailed after this. Half the dashboard is covered in neon orange dust.

"This is a fuckin' waste of time," Schaffer grumbles. "It's 2:00 a.m. We've been out here for three hours. Your C.I. was wrong. The Marquez gang ain't selling out of a place like this."

"He's solid. How the hell do you think Urbanski and I made that bust last week? It was Carter's intel that led us to that nightclub. He's a goddamn sure thing."

The radio squawks once, and Urbanski's voice fills the car. "Got movement on the south side of the building. Three white males, one with a backpack."

"Keep 'em in your sights. We're on our way." I check my SIG while Schaffer crumples up the bag of Cheetos and shoves it under the seat. He pulls a fucking wet wipe out of the pocket of his blazer and tears it open. "Are you shitting me? Urbanski is on his own out there."

"I'm faster than a duck on a June bug on my worst day," he says with a cocky smile.

"Then get a move on." I'm out of the car before he can make another smart-ass remark and halfway around the old warehouse in thirty seconds. Schaffer's light footsteps follow quickly. Maybe he ain't as slow as I feared.

Three loud *pops* sound from inside the building. I press myself to the wall, Schaffer at my side. "Dispatch, shots fired at 146th and Grand. Urbanski, Schaffer, and Blade on scene. Send backup!"

I motion for Schaffer to stick close. Where the fuck is Urbanski? We hit the door on the south side together, Schaffer yanking it open while I check for hostiles. Sweeping my gaze across the large space, I clock a handful of sleeping bags against one wall—along with a couple of shopping carts. Squatters lookin' for somewhere to stay warm.

Men and women huddle together while three guys hide behind a stack of pallets across the building, shooting at anything that moves. From the east door, Urbanski fires back. One of the asshole's bullets hits something metal close to the squatters. A man starts coughing, followed by another. "Gas!" one of them shouts.

"Get out! Move! *Vienes por aquí. Corres!*" I shout. Several shots ping off the concrete wall to my left. These idiots are going to get us all killed. "Hold your fire! You hit a fucking gas line! *No dispares!*"

"Fuck you!" a man shouts from the pallets before sending another dozen bullets my way.

Urbanski zig-zags through the warehouse, reaching the group huddled together against the wall in under ten seconds. "Go, go, go!" His voice turns hoarse. "Jas! The shutoff valve's stuck!"

"Keep 'em busy," Schaffer hisses in my ear. "I'll help Jonas."

Busy? With what? The Texas Two-Step? If I keep shooting, I could bring the whole goddamn building down. Concrete flies off the wall and slices my cheek. "You assholes are gonna die if you don't cut that shit out!"

One of them says something I can't make out over all the coughing and crying coming from the opposite side of the warehouse. Schaffer, Urbanski, and the dozen or so squatters are almost clear.

"Fucking pig!"

A burst of gunfire echoes in the dimly lit space. My ears pop. Heat washes over me. The roar is so loud, I feel it in every cell of my body. Flames lick along the ceiling.

Fuck. I'm on my back, staring up at the support beams high above me. Another dozen sharp reports pierce through the dull hum in my ears—my hearing's shot. Everything sounds like it's under water.

Those jack-offs are still shootin'.

Rolling onto my side, I fire toward where I *think* they are. Again and again until I run out of bullets. One of them staggers out from behind the pallets and collapses.

"Jas!"

Urbanski. Fuck, he sounds bad. Or maybe that's my busted eardrums. I try to get up, but my right leg won't hold my weight. The pain is unlike anything I've ever felt before. White hot and so deep, it cuts me in two.

I hit the ground. Bones crunch in my thigh. My palms are slick with blood. A couple of inches at a time, I lurch forward on my hands and knees. "Comin'. Hold...on!"

My vision's hazy. Everything to my right is dark as fuck. I reach Urbanski's side, as he starts coughing. A sharp piece of metal sticks out of his abdomen. Blood stains his lips. The side of his face is burned almost down to his cheekbone. "Did they...get out...?" he rasps.

I struggle to get close enough to hold his hand. He's dead. He knows it. It's in his eyes. The way the light's fading. The blown pupils. And the heartache in his voice.

I strain to locate Schaffer. To find any evidence of the squatters. "They're out. Stay with me, idiot. Backup is on the way."

"Tell Louann..." He gurgles as he fights for another breath. "I...love...her and the...kids."

I can't feel my right leg anymore. Or my hip. Everything's blurry as fuck, but I think I hear sirens in the distance. "Urbanski? Open your eyes, asshole. That's...a goddamn...order!"

But his entire body relaxes, and I know. He's gone.

Emi

The scent of antiseptic turns my stomach. I didn't want this story. I've only been back at work for three days. My morning passed in a flurry of phone calls—my grandmother's bank, the probate lawyer, the various charities she designated as beneficiaries of her trust. I'm drained, and it's only noon.

Grief steals so much of my energy every day. Dealing with the minutiae of death. The last wishes of the woman who practically raised me. So many decisions I never knew I'd need to make. At least we had time to prepare. But it's still exhausting.

Still, I'll be damned if I let Danny Riscaldo scoop me. It's his favorite game, and I'm sick of it. One more "Buck up, little lady, your time will come," and I'm gonna make sure he has a permanent hitch in his giddy up.

At least Nelson—Channel 5's news director—has my back.

"This could be big, Emmylou. Rumor has it, the fibbies were circling the warehouse after the explosion. Find out why. But do it quick before Danny works his contacts and freezes you out."

Gritting my teeth, I stride down the hospital corridor like I'm not about to lose my lunch all over the dull, scuffed linoleum. What did the charge nurse say? Room 762? Or Room 726? Dammit. I should have asked him to write it down.

By the time I reach Room 762, the memories are hitting hard and fast. The EMTs dragging my big sister away from me. Mama screaming at the doctors to do something. All the blood. Everything going soft and quiet, despite half a dozen people working on me at once. Dying. It didn't hurt as much as I thought it would. Coming back...that was harder.

I press a hand to my stomach to quell a burst of nausea. Twenty years, and I still can't smell antiseptic without panicking.

"Focus, Emi. You have a job to do."

My little pep talk isn't near enough. But I'm fixin' to land the biggest story to come across my desk since I moved back to Austin. I can let the abyss of my memories swallow me tonight in the darkness of my apartment.

"Eyes on the prize. Network news or bust," I whisper.

The riot inside my head settles to a dull roar. The scents of the hospital fade into the background. I can do this.

I angle a quick glance through the open door to Room 762. Lieutenant Jasper Blade—the only Texas Ranger to survive an explosion at an empty warehouse two nights ago—lies in a narrow bed with his eyes closed. His right leg is in traction, his arm in a sling held tight to his body. The side of his face looks like an angry horse dragged him ten miles over rough road.

Shit. What if he's still unconscious? The explosion was two days ago. I thought he'd be up to talking by now. But the Department of Public Safety hasn't responded to any of my calls.

"Who the fuck are you?" a man drawls.

I jerk back and almost drop my tablet. Shit. He could be Jasper's twin. His hair is darker, his face a little thinner, but they're otherwise almost identical. Stubble shadows his jaw, and as he pushes to his feet, the fluorescent lights glare off the shiny badge clipped to the double belts the Rangers so often wear.

"I'm Emmylou Marsh from Channel 5 news."

"Get out. My brother doesn't have a damn thing to say to you."

"This is a developing story. Rumor has it, the Marquez gang lost several members of their organization in that explosion. Were the Rangers investigating them? They've been linked to the Cordova Cartel on numerous occasions."

"I said, '*Get out*.'" He stalks toward me, the fire in his bloodshot blue eyes so bright, I want to look away. But this is my damn job and I'm gonna do it.

"Channel 5 was first to report on the explosion that left two decorated Rangers dead and Lieutenant Blade in critical condition. The Department of Public Safety won't comment on the investigation. What was going on at that warehouse? It hadn't been occupied for a year."

"None of your goddamn business," Jasper's brother grits out. "You want a statement, go talk to our media relations liaison."

"Surely you don't want to let speculation run wild, Ranger Blade—"

"It's Stone. *Captain* Stone. Do you think I give a shit about your...*speculation*? My brother ain't gettin' out of here for God-knows-how-long, and he sure as fuck don't want to talk to you!"

"AJ. Shut up. Or...better yet...go home." From the bed, Jasper struggles to focus on the two of us facing off in the doorway. Pain crinkles at the corners of his eyes as he lets out a shudder.

AJ flinches like someone jerked a knot in his spine, turns back to his brother, and shakes his head. "No."

"I. Don't. Want. You. Here." Each word is stronger than the last, until Jasper is practically shouting, though his voice is thick, the words slurring with exhaustion—or maybe pain.

"Well, that makes two of us. You're an asshole when you're on morphine, Jas." AJ grabs his jacket and Stetson, his voice dropping to a whisper as he adds, "And all I've got left."

Jasper doesn't react when AJ stalks out of the room. Only turns his unfocused gaze to me. "You'll have to...excuse me, ma'am. Pretty drugged up here. Mind tellin' me who you are again?"

"Emmylou Marsh with Channel 5, Lieutenant Blade." I hold out my hand, only to drop it seconds later when it clicks that the sling won't let him return the gesture.

Jasper fumbles for the bed remote, then groans as he tries to get more comfortable. The pulley system keeping his leg immobile foils his attempt. His left hand starts to shake.

"Let me help." Tucking my tablet under my arm, I snag the controller, cradle his hand in mine, and curl his fingers into position. He's warm, his skin rough and covered with tiny scratches from the explosion. "Oh, shit. Did I hurt you?"

"No, ma'am," he manages through gritted teeth. "Breathin' does that all on its lonesome."

In another few seconds, he's raised the bed enough for us to have a conversation, but the effort cost him. With a sigh, his eyes drift closed.

I should let him rest. But if I go back to the newsroom with nothing, Danny will never let me live it down. And it'll be that much harder for me to convince *anyone* I belong in a more competitive market.

Sinking down into the chair AJ was using, I cross my legs at the ankles and balance my tablet on my knee. Before I can finish searching for "AJ Stone," Jasper coughs weakly.

"Sorry," he rasps. "Can't stay awake for shit."

"Lieutenant Blade, I don't want to—"

"Jasper." His chapped lips twitch into what might be a frown. "Not...on the job at the moment." After another long pause with his eyes mostly closed, he clears his throat. "You said...Emery? Emily?"

"Emmylou Marsh. Emi."

"Emi. I'd shake your hand, but..." Jasper nods toward his right arm with a heavy sigh. "If Media Relations won't talk to you, I shouldn't either."

I flash him one of my practiced smiles and hope he doesn't notice the grief lingering in the depths of my eyes. "Then why haven't you kicked me out already?"

"Spent all my piss and vinegar on my brother." His words start to slur. "Can't see much...at the moment, but you're...a prettier sight than these walls."

A flush creeps up my neck. It's my job to look good. Always put together. Perfect makeup, perfect hair, short skirts and heels whenever I'm "on the clock." Being hit on is a daily occurrence. Sometimes even an hourly one.

Hell, there's a local subReddit where a few hundred of Austin's least respectable dude-bros post screen captures of my news reports so they can critique every outfit choice and speculate about my menstrual cycle and cup size.

But Jasper Blade doesn't seem like one of *those* guys.

I sit back and drop my facade. The perfect smile, the composure. I'm not Emmylou Marsh, on-air reporter anymore. I'm just Emi. "Is there anything you need, Lieutenant—uh, Jasper? Water? Another blanket?"

"To be able to piss standin' up." After a beat, he swears under his breath. "Fucking hell. Sorry. My head is killin' me and my filter's broke as fuck."

"Concussion? How close were you to the blast?" Concern softens my tone. I shouldn't push him. The man almost died.

"Not close enough," he whispers. "You should go."

"Jasper, if I go back to my news director with nothing, he'll give this story to Danny Riscaldo. He's a misogynistic, sanctimonious ass who thinks he's better than everyone else at the station. Is there *anything* you can tell me? What were you, Matt Schaffer, and Jonas Urbanski doing at that warehouse in the middle of the night?"

The shift in his expression is almost instantaneous. Tension stiffens his entire body. He wraps his fingers around the bed rail and pulls himself up a little straighter. "Schaffer and Urbanski were two of the bravest men I knew, *Ms. Marsh*. They got thirteen civilians out of that warehouse before it blew—while under fire. Urbanski died in my arms. You want a story? Report on them."

His sudden burst of strength fades away, and he collapses against the pillows. "I'm done talkin'. Leave. Now."

"I'm sorry, Jasper. Truly." I can't get out of here fast enough. Some days, I hate the person my job requires me to be. Today is one of them.

CHAPTER ONE

Present Day

Jasper

CRACKING open my second beer of the afternoon, I sink into my recliner. On TV, the Austin Ropers take the field to a roar of applause. They're in Denver this week, and snow flurries almost obscure the yard lines. It's gonna be a messy game.

My right leg aches—the bone-deep pain that keeps me up almost every night—and I drape an ice pack over my thigh.

Fuckin' A, that burns like a sombitch.

I should be used to it by now. Eight weeks bouncing between the hospital and rehab, multiple surgeries, months of physical therapy, and a lifetime of chronic pain to look forward to. The PT released me with a good luck handshake and a warning not to "overdo it."

My *retirement* party—if you can call the commander handing me a gold watch and saying, "See you around, Jas," a party—left me without a job or a reason to get up in the morning.

The monotony is gonna do me in—especially now, as the days march toward winter. At least in summer, the blessed relief of baseball kept me busy. I spent a chunk of change on season tickets to the Austin Stars where I could sit out in the sun and forget I'm damaged goods.

The explosion that ended my career left me with an artificial hip, three pins in my femur, a rotator cuff that's seen better days, a handful of scars decorating my right cheek, and only partial sight out of that same eye.

The Ropers gain thirty yards, and another swig of beer goes down easy. Too easy. I should switch to water. But...why? It only took me ten days to dump the pain pills. Seen too many guys get addicted to that shit and lose everything. But the alcohol? That's manageable. At least for now.

Deep down, I know I have a problem. I'm going dry in the new year.

The phone rings, rattling on the side table. I set the bottle down and swipe across the screen. "Yeah?"

"Is this the super?" the quiet male voice asks. Tim. He knows damn well who he's talking to, but he starts every call the same way.

"Yep. What broke this time, Tim?"

"The heater. It's making this terrible noise and it stinks. Like something died in here."

I stifle my groan as I push to my feet, limp into the kitchen, and toss the ice pack in the freezer. "I'll be up in five minutes. Turn it off, okay?"

"Yes, sir." The kid hangs up before I can tell him not to call me "sir."

When the building owner, Rick, found out I'd been forced to retire from the Rangers, he took pity on me and offered me this job. Handle routine maintenance for the small, thirty-unit apartment complex, collect checks for him, and he knocks my rent down to five hundred a month. Not a bad gig. Normally, a two-bedroom place like mine in downtown Austin would be four or five times that. The building's in decent condition, but it's old, so *something* goes ass up at least three or four times a week.

Before I grab my toolbox, I make a pitstop in the bathroom for some mouthwash. Rick probably won't care that I started drinking a little after 3:00 p.m. Tim either. But there's no need to flaunt it.

Pride won't let me take the elevator, so I climb two flights of stairs to the top floor and knock on the door of Unit 503.

The kid—hell, he's got to be twenty-five, hardly a kid anymore—answers and hunches his shoulders. "Sorry for the bother, Mr. Blade."

"This is my job. Unless you've been pouring concrete into the heating unit, we're solid." I try for a smile, but Tim doesn't seem convinced because he darts out of my way like a scared jackrabbit.

He ain't wrong about the stench. The whole apartment smells like the Louisiana Bayou in July, and it's colder than all get out in here. "Just how long has this been goin' on?"

"Um, three days?"

"Fuckin' A. Next time don't wait so damn long. You're lucky you're healthy. If your mama had been visitin', she could have come down with pneumonia. Plus, smells to me like the whole unit's toxic." When I crouch down in front of the main vent, a gust of moldy air hits me square in the face, and I can't stifle my grunt.

The beer isn't doing me any favors. I land on my ass with a string of obscenities rarely heard from anyone but construction workers and long-haul truckers.

"Mr. Blade! You okay?" Tim approaches cautiously, but I wave him back.

"Fine," I grit out. "But this whole unit's FUBAR. We might have a couple extras in the basement. Got any old towels lying around?"

He nods, his blond hair so long, it brushes his shoulders with the motion, and by the time he returns with an armful, I've managed to loosen the brackets holding the unit in place.

Tim spreads towels over the floor, catching the brackish water dripping from the heater. Fuck. I have to call Rick. This apartment ain't safe until we get a mold inspection done.

I wipe my hands on my jeans. Big mistake. They're toxic now too.

"Listen, Tim. I'm gonna take care of this, but do you have anywhere you can go for a couple of nights?"

"Go?" He gapes at me for a full thirty seconds before snapping his jaw shut. The shell-shocked glaze to his eyes fades, and he shakes his head. "Uh...most of my friends are back in Dallas. But..."

Shit. The poor kid's starting to spiral. I barely remember being that naive. That unwilling to believe the world is as fucked up as it really is. Defeat has him taking a step back with a heavy sigh.

"We need to get a mold specialist in here in case whatever up and died in this piece of shit has spread. Stay in a hotel for a couple of nights. The owner will comp your rent while the apartment's being inspected and we make sure it's still safe. It'll be enough for one of those extended stay places with a little kitchen, at least. Pack a bag and get the heck out of here. I'll call you when I know how long we'll need."

Thankfully, the kid doesn't argue. Just heads for his bedroom, and I hear the distinct sound of a suitcase being unzipped. Rick runs a good complex, despite the age of the building. Clean, solid, up to code. He doesn't skimp on his residents' safety. But damn. If Tim hadn't called when he did...this could have been a lot worse.

TWO HOURS LATER, Tim's got a hotel room a couple of miles away, and the apartment windows are wide open while the mold inspector does his thing.

"You're lucky. The only bad spots are around the window. You'll get by with a Level II cleaning. Takes about four hours." He taps his phone screen a couple times. "I can fit you in tomorrow at noon. That work?"

"Yep. I'm in Unit 301. Stop there first and I'll let you in."

It takes me another few hours to make sure we have a replacement heating unit ready to go, file my incident report, and finish the paperwork Rick needs to reimburse Tim for his hotel room. By 10:00 p.m., all I want is the rest of that beer and my bed.

But the Shiner is warm and flat. The pain has gone from a dull ache to electro-shock therapy. I give up on any hope of sleep.

Settling back into my recliner with a fresh, cold bottle, I take a swig. If I'm lucky, unmitigated exhaustion will eventually carry me away. If not...it's gonna be a long ass night.

Emi

I pace, *willing* the phone to ring with every fiber of my being. The carpet is still damp from cleaning, boxes are piled on the credenza and the only thing on my desk besides my laptop is the photo of me and my grandmother from my college graduation.

It's only been two days since I moved my things from a cubicle in the station's noisy bullpen. I taped a piece of paper over Danny Riscaldo's nameplate this morning. Calling Miss Up-And-Coming Austin "a pretty little thing" on air—to her face—was the final straw for the station. They fired him last week. Half the women working here had a party the day he left. This wasn't the way I wanted the cushy corner office with its big windows and room for a couch, but I sure as hell ain't gonna turn it down.

Three brisk raps on the door stop me in my tracks. Nelson, my news director, pokes his head in a second later. "Got a minute?"

Sweeping a lock of hair behind my ear, I frown and sink down into my chair. "Not much more than one or two. I have the Eugene Fowler interview on Monday. He's the owner of Consolidated Investment Group. They've built huge hotel and convention complexes all over the place in the past ten years. Chicago, Detroit, Atlanta, Dallas, and now, Austin. The Empress Hotel."

"So, he's a developer. He probably goes where the money is. Austin's growing. Big time. What's the story here?" Nelson asks. "Please tell me you're not doing a softball piece on the Empress. It's a waste of your time and talent, Emi. This office—the prime spot at six o'clock—viewers trust you to bring them the big news."

I shoot Nelson a sideways glance. "Do you think I'd lock myself in *any* office—even this one—for a week straight working on something that wasn't hard-hitting news? Fowler and CIG are dirty, Nelson. My sources are close to giving me evidence of bribes —lots of them—Fowler's paid. More than *two million* over the past ten years. He takes run-down properties with high value to the community, has them condemned, and buys them for pennies on the dollar. But there's more. His mega-hotel in Chicago has been rumored to be a meeting place for the Rossi Crime Family."

Nelson whistles and shoves his hands into his pockets. "Shit, Emi. You'd better have evidence to back that up. If you even *mention* the mob, you're asking for trouble—and a visit from the FBI. Plus, Fowler will come after you—the whole station—with lawsuits faster than a jackrabbit on a caffeine bender."

My heart rate ticks up. I think my mouth even waters a little. That's *exactly* what I hope will happen. FBI involvement will practically guarantee the story goes national. "I've been doing this job a long time, Nelson, and I'm damn good at it. I know how to dot my *i*'s and cross my *t*'s."

He tosses his hands up in mock surrender. "I know that. But I wouldn't be doin' *my* job if I didn't ask. This is big. So much bigger than the drive-by shootings outside the Shop-N-Go you covered last month. How many nights do you think this'll run?"

"Three. At least. Maybe more. I sent you the rundown an hour ago. Monday, Tuesday, and Wednesday nights are a given. Thursday hinges on what happens *after* the interview."

Visions of a two-week series float through my head. All the big networks clamoring for an exclusive.

"Emi?" Nelson waves his hand in front of my face. "Did you hear me?"

"God, I'm sorry. It's been a long day. What'd I miss?" Sending him my best "forgive me" smile, I dig my fingers into my thigh under the desk to pull a fraction of my focus back to our conversation.

"I'll give you the three nights. *After* you run down your evidence with me. Does 4:00 p.m. work?"

I don't have much choice but to agree. Nelson's a good guy. A little too cautious, but then again, he's the one the execs will come down on first if Channel 5 gets sued. Still, once in a while, he tries to flex his "I'm the boss" muscles a little too much for my tastes. I'm almost ten years older than he is, and I've been working in TV news since he was knee-high to a grasshopper.

"So, what else did you need?" I ask. "You didn't come in here for my rundown. If I only have another two hours to get my presentation together before the pitch meeting, I gotta get going on it." I run a hand through my long brown hair, fingers tangling in the strands halfway down. Too many hours at my desk twirling a lock around my thumb over and over again.

Nelson shakes his head slightly, a sure sign I'm not going to like this. "Noelle Johnson came down with the flu. She's supposed to be covering the Rangers' Boots and Bling Charity Ball tomorrow night."

"No." Before he can protest, I narrow my eyes at him and double down. "Absolutely not, Nelson. I haven't taken on a lifestyle piece in ten years. Get Christy to handle it."

"Christy *is* handling it. But it's her first time on a gig like this alone. There's gonna be some important people there, and I need someone to back her up so she doesn't get in over her head. You're always saying your mentor taught you everything you know. Return the favor. Help Christy through this."

"I don't have time—"

"It's three hours out of your Saturday night. You're the only other reporter with *any* lifestyle experience not currently scheduled to go on air Saturday. Please? You gotta eat anyway, and this is a five-hundred-dollar-a-plate dinner. Go and make sure Christy asks the right questions."

Nelson slips back out the door before I can refuse, calling over his shoulder, "I sent the details to your inbox. You're the best, Emi! I owe you one!"

Yes, he does. And if I have to cash in that chit to get the Fowler story on the air, I'll do it.

CHAPTER TWO

Jasper

I DUMP the empty beer bottle into the recycle bin and reach into the fridge for another. My fingers slip off the neck when someone bangs on my door. Tim's early. He wasn't supposed to be here for another hour.

The mold inspector gave his apartment the all clear earlier today, and the kid said he'd come by after his shift at the Stop-N-Go to sign the last of the paperwork.

"Next time you're gonna be early, call—shit." I grip the knob hard enough, my knuckles crack and stare my brother in the face. "What the hell are you doing here?"

"Good to see you too, Jas," AJ mutters as he pushes past me. My right leg threatens to buckle, but I stifle my wince and keep hold of the door until I know I'm not going down. My twin's gaze sweeps around the apartment, landing on the single recliner poised in front of the television. "You need some new furniture."

"Why? Because I have so many visitors?" I can't keep the bitter edge from my voice. In the eight months since he walked out of my hospital room, I've only seen AJ twice. Once at the funeral for the two Rangers who died in the explosion, and once at my retirement "party."

"How the hell would I know how many visitors you have?" He ambles over to the living room window and stares out at the street below.

I shrug. "Pick up the phone once in a while. Maybe you'd find out."

"Why?" That single word holds so much emotion, the air in the room swells with the weight of it.

"Jesus, AJ. Because I'm your brother? Because it ain't good for you to be alone all the time? Because we used to be close until Grace went missin'—"

"Don't, Jas," he grits out. "Don't fucking say her name..." His shoulders slump, and he runs a hand through his black hair. It's several shades darker than mine, and one of the few differences between us. That and all of five minutes of life.

I grab his arm, forcing him to turn around to face me. "You won't tell me a damn thing about the investigation, you *never* reach out—to anyone—and from what little I hear from McGrath and Elmore, you're the grumpiest sombitch in the entire Ranger Division. Maybe *you* should try to say her goddamn name once in a while."

AJ's dark blue eyes turn frigid with rage. His fingers dig into my biceps as he shoves me up against the fridge. Beer bottles rattle inside. At least one falls over. "Shut. The. Fuck. Up."

He's shaking now, but he ain't the only bull in this pasture. I can give as good as I get. "Eight months."

"What?" He shakes his head, blinks at me, and his brow furrows.

"It's been eight months since the explosion. Seven months and three days since I turned in my badge. That's the last time I saw you. My own brother. My fucking *twin*. I lost my job, half the vision in my right eye, and my partner. And you don't care. About any of it."

He doesn't move—or even breathe—for several seconds. "Fuck you, Jas. I care."

With a snort, I sidestep him and limp awkwardly over to the recliner to lower myself down. "Coulda' fooled me." I rub my thigh, but it does little to ease the ache in my leg—or my chest. While I'll be in pain for the rest of my life, AJ lost his wife two years ago, and he'll never come back from that.

After a silence so long, the Ropers get three downs, AJ's shoulders heave. "I should have been there that night," he says quietly. "Hell, it should have been *me* who died. Not Schaffer and Urbanski."

"Fucking hell, no." I spin the La-Z-Boy around and sit up straighter. "We'd been tracking those cartel assholes for two months."

"Yeah, and then Commander Ramsey suspended me for insubordination." He leans against the breakfast bar, all the bravado gone from his voice.

"You were tryin' to find your wife. That suspension was bullshit." I rub the back of my neck, squeezing hard to try to relieve some of the tension before I lurch to my feet. "Sit the fuck down. You want a beer?"

"I can't stay," he mutters. "This was a mistake."

"A mistake? For fuck's sake. Why'd you really come knockin', AJ? Because it sure as shit wasn't to check up on me." I should quit being so hard on him. I can't imagine what he goes through every damn day. But he ain't the only one hurting.

"The Boots and Bling charity dinner is tomorrow night," he says, his voice flat.

My brows shoot up. "So? In case you forgot, I'm retired."

"I didn't forget, asshole. They present the Thomas Distinguished Service Award at the ball every year. I...uh...they're awarding it to me for the Manchester case. This...came in the mail the other day." He digs into the pocket of his sport coat and withdraws a thick card.

I run my fingers over the embossed lettering across the front.

Captain AJ Stone and Mrs. Grace Stone

"Fuckin'-A. Who sent this?" I demand.

AJ shrugs. "Does it matter? What's done is done. I'm gonna

walk in there tomorrow night and the place at the table next to me is gonna have my missing wife's name on it. I can't do it alone, Jas."

The anguish on his face does me in. All my anger fades in a heartbeat. "Fine. But I ain't dancing."

THE BOOTS and Bling Charity Ball is one of the swankiest parties in town. In my ten years working for the Department of Public Safety, I only went once. Didn't much care for schmoozin' or politickin'. But AJ's only missed one in the last thirteen years—the event right after Grace disappeared.

Most of the men are in tuxes, the women in fancy gowns and heels so high, I wonder how they can walk in 'em. "Shit. There must be two hundred people here," I mutter and tug at my jacket. My black Wranglers and boots were the wrong choice.

"Two-hundred-and-six," a woman says from behind me. The voice is familiar. Silky smooth, confident. Sexy. Maybe this night won't be entirely miserable.

I turn, and my smile falters. Fuck. A stunning brunette stares right past me, her gaze sweeping over the crowd.

Emmylou Marsh. Star reporter for Channel 5 News. Does she remember me? We met. Once. Those few minutes are foggy from all the pain meds they had me on after the explosion, but I remember her beauty. And the sadness in her eyes.

Tonight, red silk drapes her curves, dipping low between her breasts. Fuck me. She's even *more* beautiful now.

Don't stare, idiot. She'll think you're a creeper.

I force my gaze up. Long, wavy brown locks tumble over her shoulders. She brushes away an errant curl, then pauses to fiddle with a silver teardrop earring dangling almost all the way to her shoulder.

Before I can offer her my hand, she waves to someone across the room and, with a quick, "Enjoy your evening," glides away on heels so thin, they should be registered as weapons.

AJ sidles up next to me, his frown etched even deeper than usual. "What the fuck? Was that...?"

"Emmylou Marsh? Yeah." I shove my hands into my pockets and hunch my shoulders. AJ might be grumpy as a hornet, but he's wearing a black suit, crisp white shirt, and a dark red tie. Next to him, my well-worn leather jacket, button-down, and black Wranglers make me look like I just wandered in from the street.

"She apologize to you?"

I stare at my brother, and a headache starts to throb between my brows. "For...?"

"Marching into your hospital room and demandin' you reveal details of an internal DPS investigation less than forty-eight hours after you flatlined on the table?" Streaks of silver flare in his eyes. "She's an ambulance chaser in a pretty dress, nothin' more."

"And you would know...how? I seem to recall, you *left*. Did you stay two hours? Three?" I snort. "Comin' here was a mistake."

AJ grabs my arm before I can stalk away. "Two *hours*? Try two days. You were hopped up on so much morphine, you had no idea what the fuck was goin' on. I was in that chair watchin' over you for two solid days, Jas. *And* nights."

The pain in his voice shocks me into silence for so long, he shakes his head. "Forget it. We need to find our seats. Dinner's startin' soon."

He wades into the crowd, toward tables set with fancy plates and sparkling crystal. Most of my first few days in the hospital were lost to whatever the fuck they gave me to ease the pain of my injuries—along with my grief and a truly unhealthy amount of guilt.

In truth, I don't remember *talking* to Emmylou Marsh. She's a hazy, angelic vision in my mind. I didn't watch the news coverage of the explosion either. But I do remember the touching tribute she delivered to Schaffer and Urbanski on the evening news the day of their funerals.

She'd taken the time to interview their friends and families. Even got the Commander to give a statement. Donations for the

Texas Rangers Association skyrocketed that day—and every day for the next week when the story was replayed on Channel 5.

Schaffer's family was able to keep their home because of those donations. And Urbanski's kid will go to college next year on a scholarship from the TRA. Unlike my brother, I don't have beef with Emmylou Marsh. Even if I should.

A man hustles up on stage and grabs the microphone. "Attention, everyone. Dinner will be served in twenty minutes. Please start making your way to your seats."

Guess I should get to findin' AJ. It doesn't take long. He's at the table closest to the stage, his entire body ramrod straight, hands clenched into fists at his sides. Those damn place cards. If someone really did put Grace's name on one...they're gonna have to deal with me.

I rest my hand on his shoulder, peering down at the table. Yup. Someone done fucked shit right up. I snatch the little white card reading *Grace Stone* from the plate, but before I can tear it into tiny pieces, AJ grits out, "Give it to me."

"No. This ain't right."

"I don't care," he says, his voice measured. "Hand it over. Right now."

It's his "I'm five minutes older and I'll never let you forget it" tone. I pass him the fancy card, and he stares at it before tracing each letter with his index finger.

"I'm gonna find out who's responsible for this and—"

"Forget it. We're here. Sit down."

I'd lay into him for his attitude, but who the fuck decides it's appropriate to set a place for a woman who's been missing for more than two years?

"Jasper?" Commander Harris claps me on the shoulder. "What are you doing here?"

I have to twist in my seat to peer up at the man. I lost almost forty percent of the vision in my right eye in the explosion. I'm about to tell him off for Grace's place card when AJ clears his throat. "He's my plus one."

The commander doesn't react to my brother's icy tone. He's probably used to it by now.

"So what's keepin' you busy these days?" Harris asks as he pulls out a chair for his wife, Celeste.

Collecting rent checks from broke college students.

Destroying my liver.

Counting the cracks on the ceiling above my bed.

I'm spared the embarrassment of answering when our host for the evening returns to the stage. "Ladies and gentlemen, please give it up for the Austin Chamber Ensemble. They'll be providin' the musical accompaniment tonight. Dinner is about to be served!"

CHAPTER THREE

Emi

FIVE-HUNDRED-DOLLAR-A-PLATE DINNER, my ass. I can't stomach another bite of the rubberized chicken, lumpy mashed potatoes, and overcooked green beans. If I'd stayed home, I'd be in a pair of yoga pants and a sweatshirt with my laptop and a mess of ribs from Emmitt's BBQ instead of here, still hungry, and in a dress that leaves very little to the imagination.

Next to me, Christy carries on a truly mind-numbing conversation with Senator Kelman's swimsuit-model girlfriend about Austin's chances of hosting the Miss Fifty States pageant next year.

My gaze keeps drifting to a table steps from the stage. And two men I know I've met, but for the life of me, can't place. They're related. Brothers, if I had to guess. They have the same build, the same crooked smile, the same nose. One of them is in full Ranger gear—down to the distinctive double-belt *and* his sidearm. The other is in a pair of Wranglers and looks downright miserable nursing a glass of amber liquid. Where do I know him from?

A vague memory rattles around in my head. *"AJ. Shut up."*

AJ? I dig into my bag for the event program and flip to the schedule for the evening.

Dinner - 6:30 p.m.
Speeches - 7:30 p.m.
Presentation of the Thomas Distinguished Service Award to Captain AJ Stone - 8:00 p.m.
Dancing - 8:30 p.m. - Midnight

AJ Stone. The name doesn't mean anything to me, but I pull out my phone and type in AJ's name. In seconds, I find a handful of articles about the kidnapping of Grace Stone—AJ's wife.

Grace Stone disappeared while out for a run near Lady Bird Lake. Her mobile phone and water bottle were found in a ditch, but there were no signs of a struggle. A reward of $50,000 has been offered by Grace's husband, a captain with the Department of Public Safety. Anyone with knowledge of her whereabouts should contact the Tip Line at 888-555-1212.

The woman disappeared a few weeks before my grandmother entered hospice care. Normally, I would have covered a story like this, but I was barely functional at that point.

A second article on Grace's disappearance includes a photo of both men at the table across from me.

Captain AJ Stone and his brother, Lieutenant Jasper Blade, leave Austin PD after the investigation into the disappearance of Captain Stone's wife was suspended. Grace Stone has been missing for three months. There have been no leads as to her whereabouts.

Jasper Blade. Shit. Now I remember. The explosion down on Grand. Jasper almost died. Nelson sent me to Austin General to get an interview out of the man. But he had a broken leg, his arm in a sling, and so many cuts and bruises I hardly recognize him now. He kicked me out of his hospital room before I could get anything out of him. Not that I blamed him. He'd just lost two of his fellow Rangers.

I'm torn between marching right over there to apologize and making a quiet exit before he remembers who I am. If he hasn't already.

Reporters *have* to push for answers. Otherwise, the news would be nothing but vague stories no one would bother watching. In my thirteen years, I've made more than my fair share of people cry. But I've rarely felt the level of guilt I did after trying to interview Jasper. The sadness—and downright despair—in his eyes that day stuck with me for weeks. I *had* to cover the death of his partner, the investigation, the potential connection to the Cordova Cartel. That was the job. But every report left me with a mountain of regret and a sick feeling in the pit of my stomach. It didn't go away until I did the human-interest story on the Rangers who lost their lives in the blast.

"Matt Schaffer and Jonas Urbanski were two of the bravest men I knew. Urbanski died in my arms. You want a story, Ms. Marsh? Report on them."

"I need some air," I say—not that Christy hears me—and beeline for the hotel lobby. It's cooler out here, with the scent of lilies perfuming the air. The Five Points went all out for this shindig, and large vases of flowers adorn almost every horizontal surface.

Finding a quiet corner, I lean against the wall and check my email. Half a dozen news alerts on my name, some SPAM, and a message from *John A. Doe* with several attachments.

"Yes!" I allow myself the smallest fist pump as I scroll through the photos. Evidence of three separate bribes Eugene Fowler paid to one of Austin's building inspectors six months ago.

God, I'd give anything to get out of here and back to my laptop to cross-check these photos with bank statements and tax records. I *could* sneak out. Christy can handle this puff piece. All she needs to do is interview a few of Austin's local celebrities. She's halfway there with Senator Kelman and his girlfriend. Surely she'll be able to find one or two others.

I have the coat check in sight when guilt slows my steps. Dammit. I had to give her a pep talk in the ladies room five minutes after I arrived tonight. While she dry heaved over one of the sparkling toilets.

With a sigh, I turn, but my toe catches on one of those infernal plastic cord covers running across the carpet. Off balance, I flail my arms, searching for something—anything—I can grab onto. My fingertips graze one of the large glass tables against the wall, but it's too far away to save me from going down.

A strong arm wraps around my waist, and I'm yanked against a hard chest. "Easy there. You okay?"

"Fine," I manage, though my heart is thumping half out of my chest. Turning, I peer up into Jasper's warm blue eyes. God, he smells like leather and whiskey and I want to live in the scent. "Lieutenant Blade—"

"Not anymore." All that warmth fades in a single blink. Jasper steadies me for another beat, his hand lingering on my hip, then takes a step back. "Watch those heels tonight, Ms. Marsh."

He does remember me. Not fondly, though. I should walk away. Leave the man to his demons—whatever they are. But instead, I wrap my fingers around his wrist and hold on. "Wait. Please? I'd like to talk to you."

Jasper drops his gaze to my siren red nails resting against his tanned skin. "I need a drink," he mutters. "But no one's stopping you from followin' me to the bar."

Despite his uneven gait, he strides back into the banquet hall with a purpose I never see outside of law enforcement or the military. I have to rush to keep up with him. He's got to be at least eight inches taller than I am.

Half a dozen people line up at the cash bar. Jasper rubs his right hip in long, slow strokes, then drags his hand through his dark brown hair. Scars etch his right cheek, down his neck, and disappear under the collar of his black button-down shirt.

"Thought you were on the crime beat," he says, his stare boring straight through me.

"I am. Mr. Blade—"

"Get the fuck away from my brother!" AJ Stone tries to get between us, and I take two quick steps back so I don't topple over. "Jas, you all right?"

"For fuck's sake." Jasper shoots his brother a look I can't quite read. "Last time I checked, I was still a grown-ass adult. Go back to the table. They're gonna call your name soon."

The two brothers face off for a moment, tension drawing tight between them, before AJ shakes his head. "Fine. Don't know why I even bother…"

Jasper's gaze follows AJ as he stalks back to the head table. "Sorry about that. My brother has a two-by-four permanently lodged up his ass."

I stifle my chuckle in case that big stick has something to do with his missing wife. That's a story I want to dig into—later. It'd make a great human-interest piece. Might even be award worthy. Handsome Texas Ranger tragically loses his wife, spends his nights alone, no leads, no hope of finding her…

Oh, God. Stop, Emi. You've caused this family enough pain.

Jasper steps closer, bringing his scent along with him, and pulling my thoughts back to the present. My body's reaction to him is…unexpected. I've never been one to swoon. Hell, I haven't gone on a single date in three years. I can't afford the distraction. My vibrator does me just fine. But those eyes…are staring at me like he's waiting for some sort of answer.

Shit. Two-by-four. Up the ass.

"I've dealt with worse," I say, flashing Jasper one of my practiced smiles.

"He's five minutes older than I am. When we were comin' up together…" he shakes his head with a faraway look in his eyes, "he used to think it was his mission in life to protect me. Until I kicked his ass in one of our trainin' courses, and he broke his arm. That put me three months ahead of him."

"And then it was *your* job to protect *him*?" I ask.

Jasper snorts. "Hardly. I was a fuck-up when I started out. AJ was made for this job. Probably why he's still doin' it."

The guy ahead of us ambles off with his Shiner. Jasper's hand rests lightly on the small of my back for a brief moment before he jerks his arm away.

"What'll it be?" the bartender asks.

"Whiskey. Neat. Make it a double. And whatever Ms. Marsh wants."

"Club soda with lime." I offer Jasper a small smile. "I'm technically working."

"Here?" His sudden concern is almost comical. "You ain't about to tell me AJ's under investigation, are you?"

My laugh eases some of the tension currently turning his shoulders into twin slabs of granite. "No. Nothing like that. I was one of the few reporters without an on-air segment tonight. I drew the short straw. Christy McKnight—she's Channel 5's style reporter—is covering this event, but it's her first solo gig." I nod toward our table in the center of the room. Thank God. She finally has her notebook out in front of her. "I'm her backup. Her mentor. Or both."

"Is she even old enough to drink?" Jasper digs a twenty-dollar bill out of his back pocket and slides it across the bar.

"Christy? She's twenty-four." I frown. She has a glass of champagne in her hand. Dammit. She knows better than that. If anyone catches her drinking on camera, her story won't hold *any* weight. Not that she'll get much of a scoop here.

"Here's your club soda, ma'am," the bartender says. "And sir? Your whiskey."

Jasper takes a healthy swig of his drink, while I manage only a small sip of mine. I should go tell Christy to dump the bubbly. But then Jasper's hand hovers close enough to my back that I can feel the heat of him, and I let him guide me over to the wall where we're out of the way but can still see the stage.

"Say what you got to say, Ms. Marsh. But make it quick. As soon as AJ gets his award, I'm outta here."

Now that's an interesting tidbit. Why wouldn't he stick around? My thoughts start to spiral. They're clearly not close. Yet Jasper came to the gala as AJ's plus one.

I have to stop. Not *everything* is a story. If I don't tell Jasper how sorry I am now, I might not get another chance.

"Mr. Blade, I owe you an apology. Showing up in your hospital room after...well, after you..."

"Lost everything?" He takes another gulp of his whiskey, then shudders from the burn of the alcohol. "Ain't no never mind, ma'am. The way I see it, you were just doin' your job."

"That doesn't make it right." I can't stomach any more of the club soda, and set it on a tray next to us. It's terrible. Bitter as sin and twice as flat. "I pushed you hard enough you threw me out. Then I did the one thing you told me not to do. I reported on the connection between the Cordova Cartel and the Marquez drug ring."

"Don't remember much of that day," Jasper says with a slow shake of his head. "Didn't watch the news for a solid week after. So whatever you did or didn't do...can't say I care, Ms. Marsh."

Across the room, the emcee takes the stage to a round of applause. I glance at Christy, happy to see her writing in her note-book—*not* drinking—and when I turn back to Jasper...he's gone.

Jasper

I should have walked out five minutes after AJ accepted his award. Then I wouldn't be trapped at this table babysitting my big brother while he nurses a single glass of tequila. The *same* glass of tequila he's been staring into for the past hour.

The commander asked his wife to dance a bit ago. The other Rangers at the table—Sergeant Parker Elmore and some new recruit named Hardison—left already. They're working tomorrow, and it's nearly 10:00 p.m.

"We could bail." I finish my third whiskey of the night—not my smartest decision, even if it is a necessary one—and stare back at the cash bar. A fourth might keep the pain at bay. But it'll leave me with one hell of a hangover. Dammit. I promised myself I'd be better. Time to switch to water.

"You go. If I leave now, I'll never hear the end of it." He brings the rocks glass to his lips and inhales.

"I reckon tequila works better when you actually *drink* it."

With a sigh, he shakes his head. "This...ain't for me."

Then who the hell is it—? Goddammit.

Grace. Tequila was always *her* drink.

I sit up a little straighter and set my glass down. "AJ, come on.

You need an excuse to leave? Tell Commander Harris I'm lit and you're takin' me home. I'll even act the part."

He gives me the side-eye. "You *are* lit, Jas. You're just damn good at hidin' it."

"Fuck you. I came, didn't I?" Shoving my chair back, I push to my feet and wince as my right knee threatens to buckle. "You can go back to ignorin' me now. See you in a year. Or...never."

He doesn't look up. The memories in that glass mean more to him than I ever did.

By the time I get outside, I'm halfway to forgiving him. Probably a side effect of the whiskey. AJ's gone through hell for almost two years. He's earned that stick up his ass. But would it kill him to take it out for five fuckin' minutes?

My rideshare app claims the nearest car is forty-five minutes away. Shit. I knew I should have left hours ago.

I won't make it home on foot. Not with my bum leg. My apartment is three miles from here. And goin' back inside? Fuck that. The coffee shop on the corner is open late. At least there, I can sit alone and sober up. Maybe by the time I get home, I'll be so exhausted, it won't matter how much pain I'm in.

But when I push through the door, the first thing I see is a pair of crimson fuck-me heels.

Turn around, Jas. Right now.

But, I can't. Slowly, I lift my gaze. Toned, tanned legs, red silk clinging to a tight ass, and long brown locks. Emmylou Marsh stands at the counter staring up at the menu.

"I'll have a cappuccino with almond milk," she says. "Make it a double shot." A car honks out on the street, and Emi tosses a glance over her shoulder. All the color drains from her cheeks. "Mr. Blade? What are *you* doing here?"

Shit. I shove my hands into my Wranglers. "Waitin' for my rideshare somewhere my brother's foul mood won't rub off on me. Don't worry. I ain't followin' you."

"Oh. I didn't think—"

The left side of my mouth curls up into a half smile. "You sure? That look on your face says otherwise."

Emi blushes, her cheeks almost the same color as her dress now. "I'm sorry. It was a long evening, and it's going to be an even longer night of work when I get back to the office." Tucking a lock of hair behind her ear, Emi beckons me up to the counter. "You bought my drink earlier. The least I can do is buy yours now."

"You don't have to—"

"I do. What'll it be, Mr. Blade?"

I sidle up to the register. Damn. She's only inches away from me, and those chestnut eyes of hers are mesmerizing. "Call me Jasper. I'll take a coffee. Black. No room for cream."

"Now that's the drink of a man who doesn't believe in joy. Or doesn't sleep much." She passes her phone over the card reader. "Which one are you, Jasper?"

"Both, I reckon." The urge to tell her why I don't sleep shouldn't be this strong. I barely know the woman. But there's something about her. Or maybe that's all the whiskey talking.

"Do you want to sit down?" Emi asks once the barista hands us our drinks. "The hotel valet was so busy, they said it would be at least twenty minutes before they could get to my car."

"I've got some time." I gesture for her to pick a table, and she leads me to one next to the window, angling her chair so she can see the front of the hotel—and presumably her car when it shows up.

Lifting the to-go cup, she takes a sip of the cappuccino. A spot of foam dots the corner of her mouth. Watching the tip of her tongue dart out to flick it away is practically a religious experience.

Fuck. Get your act together. You ain't lookin' to start something.

The scent of the dark brew grounds me. "Your boss sends you to a fancy party and then expects you to work all night? On a Saturday?" I ask.

Her laugh sends blood shooting right to my dick.

"I *should* go home," she says with a little shrug. "But I have a big interview on Monday that I need to prepare for. At the office, I'm less likely to fall asleep mid-email."

"What kind of interview?" I keep my tone casual—just making conversation—though I'm desperate to know more about her.

"That's a secret. If it goes well, you'll find out when the rest of Austin does. Monday night at 6:12 p.m. Give or take." Her smile lights up her entire face. Lips parted, pupils dilated, a flush creeping up her neck... She's genuinely excited. Giddy, even.

I raise a brow, aiming my own grin her way. "Are you good at secrets, Emi?"

Her top teeth sink into her bottom lip and she fixes me with a heavy-lidded gaze. "Secrets come with the job, Jasper. And I'm *very* good at my job."

A spark of awareness rushes up my spine. Is she flirting with me? Or is the booze throwing off my radar? Before I can settle on an answer, she's on her feet. "There's my car." Her fingers sweep lightly over my shoulder as she scoots past me, and I feel it down to my marrow. "This was nice. I'll see you later, Mr. Blade."

It takes a shit ton of effort to stop myself from turning to watch her go. Instead, I smile into my next sip of coffee. "Here's hopin', Ms. Marsh."

CHAPTER FOUR

Emi

SSUNLIGHT GLINTS off the windows of the steel-and-glass monolith that will soon be the Empress Hotel and Conference Center. Blinded for a moment, I don't see the errant rock in my path, and I almost go down for the second time in twenty-four hours. Not the impression I want to make on the owner of Consolidated Investment Group. This could be the biggest interview of my career.

But Eugene Fowler is distracted, his phone to his ear, talking in hushed tones. From the set of his shoulders, the conversation isn't going well. Poor Eugene. If he thinks he's having a bad day now...

I scan the expansive construction site, looking for the best place to set up. My cameraman, Kyle, points to the southwest corner of the half-finished hotel tower. "The light there should be perfect, Emi."

"Great. Get some wide shots of the conference center—all the glass windows on the west side, the guys pouring concrete, and the signage—while I prep Fowler. He's gonna need some ground rules."

With a chuckle, Kyle hefts the camera onto his shoulder as Eugene turns and adjusts his big, silver belt buckle like it's tied directly to his dick. Years of experience keep me from saying a word, though the urge to roll my eyes is almost overwhelming.

Breathe, Emi. If he wants to play at being a big-time Texan—even though he's only been here two years—let him. It'll make for a better story.

Heaven help me. He pinches the ends of his handlebar mustache with a wink, then ambles over like he owns the whole damn world.

"Mr. Fowler, it's a pleasure," I say with a smile wide enough, my lips would crack if I were allowed to let them. On-air reporters have to maintain decorum, after all. And certain *physical standards.*

Fowler's gaze trails down my body, pausing—of course—on my breasts. The white silk shirt and push-up bra do a damn good job of making me look a fair bit younger than my forty years. He stops again at the hem of my skirt—and my legs, bare from just above the knee down to my black pumps.

"Well, ain't you just the prettiest thing," he says as he leans in to peck my cheek.

I take a step back before his lips touch my skin, but keep the smile plastered in place. "Why thank you, Mr. Fowler. But I can't mess up my on-screen make-up." Gesturing behind me, I continue. "My cameraman, Kyle, will need about fifteen minutes to get some B-roll, and then we'll get started. While he's working, let's go over the questions I'll ask you. That sound good? Oh, and Cheri here is going to make sure you look perfect."

His beady eyes narrow. Did he think he was camera ready? Hardly. His cheeks are shinier than a newly minted penny.

After a beat, he gets himself under control. "Of course, little lady. You're in charge."

Yes. Yes, I am.

"When we're on-air, I must insist you call me Emmylou or Ms. Marsh. Station rules, I'm afraid." At his hardening expression, I quickly add, "You don't mind, do you, sugar?"

He's clearly *not* from Texas or he'd know "sugar" isn't a term of endearment. Anyone born and raised here knows it means "idiot." But it does the job. While I hate—*hate*—using the little tricks women in my position have been relying on for decades, I'm not above them. Not for a story like this. And Fowler doesn't know what's coming for him.

As if God himself agrees with me, Eugene chuckles. "Not at all. I'm putty in your pretty little hands."

Ick.

Cheri, the perky redhead who does my makeup, approaches Fowler with a container of pressed powder and a brush. "Mind if I just tone down those cheeks a bit?" she asks.

"You can do whatever you want to me, darlin'." His wink turns my stomach. From the look on Cheri's face, she's right there with me. But she's been in this industry almost as long as I have. She knows how to hold her tongue.

At least in Los Angeles, the guys had the decency to be *a little* sly about their chauvinism. They'd talk behind my back, occasionally let a hint of derision slip into their voices, but if I called them on it, they'd apologize faster than a duck on a June bug.

I'd give anything to return to the city of angels, but I'm stuck here until I get a story juicy enough to catapult me back into the national spotlight.

Turns out, leaving Los Angeles for a job in Texas—even if I had no choice—is a career-ending move. Unless I get my ass in gear. One story big enough to make it all the way to the national news cycle and stay there for at least a month, and I'm back in the game. Otherwise, I'm a "has-been." An *old* has-been, even at only forty. In television news, that's ancient.

But this story? I'm crossing my fingers *and* toes. Hell, I'd find a way to cross my eyelashes if that weren't against company policy. If I'm right—and I've done enough research to *know* I am—this is my ticket back to the big leagues.

With my smile in place, I return my focus to Fowler and flip open my notebook. The man's big. At least six feet tall and carrying an extra hundred pounds on his bulky frame. Hazel eyes, a close shave outside of the mustache. And looking for all the world like he's completely and totally in control. I wonder how long that will last?

"So, we'll start out with a little history of Consolidated Investment Group. How long you've run the company, some of your past projects, and what inspired you to choose this spot for the Empress Hotel and Conference Center, okay?" I glance down at the little notebook, then back up at him. The neatly printed text on the page is mostly for show—and to give me something to look at before I flutter my eyelashes at the disgusting ass in front of me. That move should spur him into answering any question.

"Whatever you think is best," he says, his voice oozing with charm as he casually brushes Cheri's ass with the back of his hand. She adds just a bit too much powder to one of his cheeks in retaliation, and God. I love her. She knows just how far to take her revenge. "As long as I can mention the shindig we're throwin' to raise money for the new youth center next month."

"Oh, of course, sugar." Like I'd forget *that*. It's the whole reason I'm here.

"We're all ready to go Emmylou," Kyle says as Cheri pins the wireless microphone to Eugene's suit jacket.

"Now remember, Mr. Fowler, this is a live interview, so try to keep the cussing to a minimum," I offer with a sweet smile. "Otherwise, we'll have to bleep you, and we certainly don't want to do that."

Eugene chuckles and tugs at his dark suit coat. "I'm sure we'll be just fine, little lady." With another wink, he adds, "Ms. Marsh."

Kyle gives me the silent countdown, and I take a slow, centering breath.

You can do this. Don't back down. Get him to crack, and you're golden.

"This is Emmylou Marsh reporting from the future site of the Empress Hotel and Conference Center. With me, I have Eugene Fowler, owner of Consolidated Investment Group, and the driving force behind the development of the Empress."

For two full minutes, we stick to the script Fowler expects, and he's getting comfortable—both with me and with being on camera.

"This site *was* rather controversial, Mr. Fowler. For months, you had protestors demonstrating outside the fence every single day." Kyle pans the camera for a wide shot showing the mostly empty fenced lot devoid of all but a handful of construction workers and a few passersby. When the camera refocuses on me and Eugene, the man's smile has faltered slightly, but he's still on his game.

"Now that we did, Ms. Marsh. We had to tear down a youth center on the northeast corner of the property, and the community was understandably upset. But that building was infested with black mold. In fact, it was condemned not long after we broke ground. It was a miracle none of the kids came down with serious health problems." Fowler straightens his tie, his chest puffing out with pride. "In a couple of weeks, I'm hosting a charity event at the Metro Hotel on Grand. All the money we raise will go to build a brand new, state-of-the-art community center four times the size of the original. A small percentage of the profits from the Empress Hotel will fund staff and supplies for the center so any child in the city can attend its programs for free."

"That's quite generous of you, Mr. Fowler."

"I think so, little lady. But it's also the right thing to do."

Flipping a page in my notebook for effect, I narrow my eyes at Eugene. "The *right* thing? That's interesting. Was it the *right thing* to pay off the health inspector who condemned the old youth center? To the tune of fifty thousand dollars?"

Fowler's cheeks turn splotchy. "Now listen here, Ms. Marsh—"

"You also *donated* another thirty thousand to the city planner who approved your permits for the Empress. Isn't that right?"

He's full-on crimson now. "You have no basis for these wild allegations! This is libel!"

I stifle my snort. "Don't you mean slander, Mr. Fowler? Libel is for print media. But you'd still be wrong. Alan Trowing, the building inspector, sent me copies of his bank records, screenshots of the text messages the two of you exchanged, and photos of the cash *you* gave him. The serial numbers are clearly visible. Should I contact your bank and ask them if the bills were withdrawn from your account? Or perhaps the account of one of your associates?"

"Fucking bitch," Eugene snarls. "What the hell are you playing at?"

Despite the adrenaline flooding my veins, I manage to keep my expression neutral. "Playing? I'm not playing, Mr. Fowler. I'm simply reporting the facts. You only obtained the permits for the full complex because the community center was condemned. And when you *did* get those permits, you paid less than a quarter of what most developers would have been charged. I can show you the receipts."

"Now look here, missy. This was supposed to be a publicity piece on the Empress Hotel. You've turned it into a trial without judge or jury. I refuse to listen to these unfounded allegations one more second!"

He yanks the microphone off his lapel, pulls the battery pack from his pocket, and throws them right at me. The shock as they hit my side makes my placid expression falter for a second, but I catch the jumbled mess before it hits the ground.

"You'll be sorry, bitch," Fowler growls under his breath as he storms away.

Did he just...threaten me? Damn. I wish he hadn't taken the mic off.

"Well, that took a turn," I say, no longer smiling as I stare directly into the camera. "Over the next three nights, tune in for a special investigative series on Eugene Fowler, the Empress Hotel Project, and the corruption we've uncovered surrounding Consolidated Investment Group. For Channel 5 Evening News, this is Emmylou Marsh reporting."

Kyle gives me the all clear, and Cheri's at my side two seconds later. "Are you okay, Emi?"

"I'm fine. Stop fussing. We need to get back to the station. I want this story dialed in tight. A corrupt land developer *throwing his mic* at the on-air reporter and *threatening her*? This is going national. I can feel it."

CHAPTER FIVE

Jasper

"For Channel 5 Evening News, this is Emmylou Marsh, reporting."

I flip over to Monday Night Football and head for the kitchen. Emi wasn't lying about her "big story." Fowler practically threatened her before he stormed off. Piece of shit.

I could see the Empress Hotel construction site from my physical therapist's office. They tore down the old community center while I was fightin' to get my strength back on the treadmill. Every week, I had to fight my way through the protestors to get a rideshare.

Sliding a pan of frozen lasagna into the oven, I pick up my cell phone and text my brother.

Jasper: Did you watch the news tonight? Emmylou Marsh is going after that big developer, Eugene Fowler. He's dirty as fuck. You ever hear his name mentioned in the same breath as the cartel?

One of the construction workers in the background while Emi was interviewing Fowler looked a hell of a lot like the guy who shot the gas line all those months ago. I can't shake the feeling there's more to this story than bribes and kickbacks.

It's none of my damn business, but when I haven't heard from

AJ by the time the lasagna's ready, I reach out to the only other person in the Department of Public Safety who might take my call.

Parker Elmore picks up on the first ring. Without her, I wouldn't know anything about my brother anymore. During the endless days I spent in the hospital—after AJ walked out—Elmore checked up on me. Since then, we've had coffee once a month. She tells me how ornery my brother is, and I let her vent without gettin' herself fired—since AJ's her captain.

"You know anything about Eugene Fowler?"

"Well, hello to you too, sunshine," she drawls. "Who you askin' about now?"

"Eugene Fowler. The developer. Emmylou Marsh from Channel 5 is doin' a story on him. She says he's dirty as fuck."

The sounds of silverware and conversation carry over the line. "Oh, she does? And how did *you* get to talkin' with Emmylou Marsh?"

"Parker, pay attention. And get somewhere quieter. I need information." I ignore the oven timer and limp back out to the main room with my phone tucked between my shoulder and my ear.

"Fine. This better?" she asks. Now, all I hear is some light traffic. "Spill it, Jasper. Is Emmylou Marsh as beautiful in person as she is on TV?"

"She's drop dead gorgeous. But I didn't *talk* to her about Eugene Fowler. I watched her story on the six o'clock news tonight. I need to know if he has any cartel ties."

"*You* need to know? Jas, you're retired. I can't give you details on an active case. Don't ask me to."

The call drops, but I got what I needed. There *is* a case involving Eugene Fowler. I sure hope Emi knows what she's gettin' herself into.

THE LASAGNA BURNED to a crisp while I was talkin' to Elmore—and tryin' to figure out if what I learned warranted a visit to Channel 5

News. I worry Emi's in over her head, but she's a grown-ass woman —and a damn good reporter. If I try to get her to back off the story, she'd probably shove my hat somewhere the sun don't shine. I'd deserve it, too.

So I head for one of the quieter sports bars off of Sixth Street. The one with the best nachos in town.

Most of the tables are taken. There's only a single two-person booth close to the door. I'm heads down staring at the menu when a burst of cold air stirs the napkin in front of me. Seconds later, a shadow flickers in the remnants of my peripheral vision.

"Jasper?" Emi—no makeup, her hair mussed from the wind, and cheeks tinged pink—stares at me like she's seeing a ghost. "What are you doing here?"

"A man's gotta eat. Didn't expect to see you in a place like this."

Her eyes narrow. "What's that supposed to mean?"

Fuck. Boot, meet mouth. I rub a hand over my short beard with a sigh. "That I'm an ass? I just meant—"

Her laughter shocks me. "Jasper, relax. I'm off the clock. Can't you tell?" She waves her hand up and down her body, and shit. No makeup, black yoga pants and a soft blue sweater, tennis shoes... This is the *real* Emi, and she's fucking gorgeous. "I get takeout here every couple of weeks. Their enchilada plate is to die for."

I don't know whether to be relieved she ain't meeting someone or disappointed she's only here for takeout. Sweeping my gaze around the bar, I nod at the bench across from me. "Enchiladas are better hot. It's full up in here, but that seat's empty. If you'd like to join me."

Emi plays with a lock of her hair, twisting it around her index finger. "You don't mind?"

"Nope. Though, I don't get out much. Or talk to many people. My 'polite conversation' skills are a little rusty."

With a chuckle, she tosses her bag into the corner of the booth and slides in across from me. "You're in luck, then. Because I talk to people for a living. I'll ease you back into it."

Fuck. This isn't gonna end well. She's the most beautiful—and successful—woman I've met in a long damn time. One slip up, and she'll walk right out of here and never give me the time of day again.

The server comes to take our order—an enchilada plate for her and loaded nachos for me. She asks for a club soda, so I give up on the beer I was planning and stick to water.

"Saw your 'big story' tonight," I say once we're alone again. "Fowler was a real dick to you."

Emi's lips flatten. "He's the worst kind of asshole. Thinks he can buy his way into—or out of—any situation. He'll get his soon enough. When my series is done, he'll be lucky if he's not in jail for a very long time."

"You're goin' after him again tomorrow?" Worry crawls up my spine. "Emi, I think you should—"

She leans forward, something akin to desperation in her brown eyes. "Can we talk about something that's *not* my job? I've been living and breathing this story for almost a month."

Well, shit. I should tell her about my phone call with Elmore, but I can't ignore her plea. Or the emotion in her voice. "We can talk about anything you want. But remember those rusty conversation skills I mentioned?" The bar erupts into cheers, and I glance up at one of the TVs in the corner of the room. The Ropers just scored a touchdown. Sports. Sports is a safe topic. "You follow football?"

Her laugh lights up her entire face. "Only enough to joke around with the camera crew in the studio. I'm more of a baseball fan. You want to know the box scores from the last run the Austin Stars made for the World Series, I'm your girl."

"I can do baseball. Spent most of the summer at the ballpark." I rub my hand across the back of my neck. I'd been nursing a headache all day, but after ten minutes with Emi, it's almost gone. "Too bad they finished in last place."

"I'm surprised you didn't bail after the All Star break." She settles back in the booth and takes a long pull on the straw in her club soda.

Damn. I never thought something so simple could be so sexy.

"Bein' outside in the sun was worth the heartache. It was either that or never leave my apartment." The admission is easy—too easy. And too much.

Emi's brows curve up. "You're not...uh...working?" At my flinch, her cheeks flush crimson. "Oh, God. That was incredibly rude. Ignore me, Jasper. I don't have much of a filter after a big story."

"Ain't no never mind. And it's a fair question. I couldn't go back to the Rangers after...what happened. Bum leg, traumatic brain injury, and my shoulder's permanently fucked." The headache's back now, ten times worse than when I walked in here. The pity in Emi's eyes doesn't help. "I got lucky, though. The owner of my apartment building comps most of my rent in exchange for me handlin' a lot of the day-to-day maintenance issues. Between that and disability, I do okay. Just don't get out much. By choice."

"I don't either," she admits with a small smile. "Unless it's for work."

"That's hard to believe. Someone who looks as good as you did in that dress should be paintin' the town every weekend."

Another laugh—almost a snort a little too close to a sip of club soda—and Emi dabs at her bare lips with a napkin. "That sounds like the worst kind of torture. I'm an 'in bed by ten' sort of gal. Saturday night wrecked me for a full twenty-four hours. I spent all day Sunday in my pajamas working from my couch."

The server drops off our food, and I wonder just what kind of pajamas Ms. Emmylou Marsh favors. And if I'll ever get to see them.

———

THE GAME IS ALMOST over by the time I convince Emi to let me pick up the check. She argued with me for a full twenty minutes before I told her my mama would never forgive me if she found out I let a woman pay for dinner when *I'd* invited *her* to sit down.

"Can I walk you to your car?" Offering her my elbow, I fully expect her to refuse. While we've been flirtin' on and off all night, I still don't know much about her. But she wraps her fingers around my bicep with a smile.

"You're one of those honest-to-God good guys, aren't you?" she asks once we're outside. "Kind to strangers, kids, and the elderly. You rescue kittens and puppies in your spare time. Or return all the loose shopping carts to the grocery store."

"Shopping carts are a fucking menace to society," I mutter. "Don't matter how new they are, one wheel is always broken. Never thought much about getting a cat or dog while I was working, though I've got the time, now."

We reach her car—a pretty powder blue Mustang convertible —and Emi digs her keys out of her bag. "Tonight was fun, Jasper. I don't think I realized how much I needed...fun." She levers up on her toes and presses a quick kiss to my cheek. Jasmine and vanilla swirl around me, a heady, sweet scent I'll never forget. Never want to.

I hold open her door, then lean down so I can meet her gaze. "I'd like to see you again. Would you consider giving me your phone number? Or I could give you mine."

Emi pulls a small notebook and pen from her center console. "Write it down, Blade. When I'm done with this story, I'll give you a call."

I can't get the digits on paper fast enough. Our fingers brush when I hand the pen and paper over. Hers are soft and warm against my calluses. I've got it bad, and we've only spent a couple of hours together. "Get home safe, Emi. And...thanks."

"For what?" she asks as the engine purrs to life and she fastens her seat belt.

"You weren't the only one who needed...fun." I tip my hat and back away before I can tell her tonight was about more than "fun." Spending time with Emmylou Marsh reminded me that I might be damaged goods, but I'm still very much alive. And I need to start acting like it.

CHAPTER SIX

Emi

SCROLLING through the replies on Channel 5's social media accounts isn't for the faint of heart. Not after my interview with Eugene Fowler went viral.

Most of the comments are encouraging.

"Developers are always corrupt."

"The Empress is ugly as sin."

"Austin don't need another big-ass hotel. We need affordable housing!"

But a not-insignificant percentage demand we "leave poor Eugene alone."

Like I'm going to listen to anonymous keyboard warriors whining about a corrupt land developer getting his ass handed to him.

Then there are the outright threats. Comment after comment telling me to die in a fire, go fuck myself, or watch my back.

I should stop scrolling. It's not doing my sanity any good. But this is part of the job. Before the next installment of the series, I need to understand public opinion.

By the fourth page of comments, the tone has shifted entirely.

"That prissy bitch doesn't know a real man when she sees one. Maybe I'll go down to Channel 5 and show her."

"I should drop Emmylou's naked body off Reckless Ridge after I rip her to shreds with my dick."

"Watch your back, cunt. Your gonna be bent over the garbage bin begging for my cock behind News 5. I'll be their at 7."

Oh, the urge to reply and correct his usage of your and their.

My desk phone rings before I can read any further, and I close my internet browser. Enough of *that* for today.

"Emi? You have visitors waiting for you." Channel 5's receptionist, Nia, sounds distracted. Worried, even. She's usually so calm.

I check my calendar. "There's nothing on my schedule. I blocked off this whole afternoon to work on the Eugene Fowler story. Who's here? Did you get their names?"

She lowers her voice to a whisper. "Um...they say they're with the FBI. Agents Van and Spooner. They had badges and everything."

"Yes!" I can't help doing a little dance in my chair. This is exactly what I was hoping for. I already had a call with Austin PD this morning. They're supposed to get back to me before the end of the day with an update on their investigation of Consolidated Investment Group—though I don't think they'll tell me much. They can't if they expect to make a strong case against CIG and Fowler.

"Um...Emi?" Nia asks. "Are you okay? I put them in Conference Room B. They're waiting for you."

Shit. She wasn't ready for my level of excitement. "Sorry. Yes. Get the agents some coffee or tea and let them know I'll be there in two shakes. I need to see if Nelson's free to sit in."

My boss isn't in his office, so I'm on my own. Probably better that way. He'd spend the whole meeting focused on the couple dozen death threats I've received in the past two days. *I'm* not the story. Consolidated Investment Group's corruption is the story.

I breeze into the conference room with my tablet tucked under my arm. "Gentlemen. I'm Emmylou Marsh."

The two men rise almost in tandem to shake my hand. They're both on the short side. Five-eight, five-nine at most. Spooner is a broad guy, but Van's a little softer. Meeker too. Yet he's the one who speaks first.

"A pleasure, Ms. Marsh. I'm Special Agent Michael Van. That's my partner, Harlan Spooner. We'd like to ask you a few questions about Eugene Fowler and Consolidated Investment Group."

With one of my polished smiles, I sink into a chair across from them. "Of course. Anything to help the FBI."

Spooner leans back in his chair, his fingers steepled in front of his face like he's contemplating the mysteries of the universe. Van pulls a small notebook from his jacket pocket and clicks his pen.

"Ms. Marsh," Van says, his voice even. Measured. "Your coverage of Eugene Fowler and his company came to our office's attention. If what you reported is true—"

Frustration prickles along my spine. "Now hold on just a minute, Agent Van. *If* my reports are true? I have evidence. Some of my sources are confidential, but others were very willing to talk on camera."

Van frowns and glances down at his notebook. "Like Alan Trowing? One of Austin's building inspectors? We tried to interview him this morning, but at 10:00 a.m. yesterday, he called his supervisor and resigned. His mobile phone is off, and his neighbor saw him put a suitcase into his car and drive away around noon."

I don't react—years of practice let me keep my cool in the most outrageous of circumstances—but why would Trowing run? He gave me permission to use his name. He sent me photo evidence of Fowler's bribes. I fire up my tablet. "I have a signed statement from Mr. Trowing *and* copies of an email chain with his supervisor. He knew what he was doing when he admitted to taking money from Fowler and his boss agreed Trowing could take six weeks of leave —with pay—before he resigned for having the guts to come forward and admit what he'd done."

I turn the device around so the agents can see the email on screen. Spooner holds out his hand, but I shake my head.

"Sorry, gentlemen. This is as close as you get without a warrant."

"Ms. Marsh, you don't want to run afoul of the FBI," Spooner grits out.

My smile falters for a split second before I plaster it back in place. "I'm not legally required to divulge my sources," I say, keeping my voice steady. "The Empress Hotel project was controversial from the start. You've clearly watched my first two reports. Bribes, shady land deals, and illegal demolitions are only the beginning. But I think you know that."

Van's eyes narrow. "We know the third installment of your report runs tonight. Tell us what bombshell you're delivering next."

My breath catches in my throat. This is my biggest scoop yet. At least twenty-five percent of the construction workers on the Empress project aren't union members. They're criminals with ties to the Cordova Cartel and the Ricci Syndicate in Chicago. "Sorry, gentlemen. You'll have to tune in like everyone else."

"You're not this naive, Ms. Marsh." Spooner's voice is as thick and smooth as velvet wrapped around a blade. "One of your sources is missing. And your *target* is the kind of guy who makes problems disappear. Permanently."

The weight of his words settles over me. My stomach twists, but it's not in fear. It's because I know how important this story is. I can't stop now. Not until I find something that stops Fowler from moving onto another city and starting his criminal enterprise right back up again. Austin deserves better than empty promises.

"If you're asking me to back down, Agent Spooner, you're wasting your time. The people of this city count on me to report the news. So that's exactly what I'm going to do."

After a long pause, Van leans forward. His eyes bore into me like he's searching my soul. "Just remember, Emmylou. Sometimes the truth doesn't set you free. Sometimes...it makes you a target."

He's not wrong. But the truth is all I have.

IT'S another two hours before Van and Spooner finally give up. They have no legal right to force me to drop the story, and if I let myself be swayed by some nasty comments and social media threats...well...I wouldn't be able to call myself a reporter.

Nelson is waiting for me outside my office door. "We need to talk." There's enough gravel in his tone to pave a country road. I don't know that I've ever seen him this serious.

"I know, I know. I should have had Nia page you when the FBI showed up. But she said you were at a big meeting with the network and—"

"The FBI?" He shakes his head. "Jesus, Emi. I should shelve tonight's segment right now." He thrusts his tablet at me, and I peer at the email on screen.

Ms. Marsh,

You have no business calling yourself a reporter. Your latest take-down piece on Eugene Fowler is the last straw. Walk away, or you might find yourself unable to report on anything ever again.

The message is unsigned—of course—and I shake my head. "Typical."

"This doesn't phase you at all?" Nelson asks. "It's a fucking death threat, and you're looking at it like it's a recipe for sugar cookies!"

"I worked in Los Angeles for six years. Threats like this? They were as common as cornbread." I lean a hip against my desk. "I'll forward the email to the FBI, but you can't pull my next segment. Journalism 101. If someone's trying to intimidate me into backing down, I'm onto something big. So quit hollerin' down the rain and let me do my job."

Nelson sighs, the sound of a man who knows when he's met his match. "Fine. But I'm going to hire security to escort you to and from your car. Is your building safe? Is there somewhere else you can stay until the story's done?"

"I am *not* turning tail. And you absolutely will not get me a bodyguard. Folks who send messages like this are all hat and no cattle. If they were serious about taking me out, they wouldn't talk about it first, they'd just do it."

Pushing to my feet, I check my watch. "Tonight's segment airs in an hour. I need to get to make-up so I can do the intro live. I should be good for another two segments next week. Monday and Tuesday. After that, these idiots will fade into obscurity again. Well, all except for Eugene Fowler. He should be in federal custody by then." My lips curve into a small smile. "Can't wait to report on *that*."

CHAPTER SEVEN

Jasper

"THAT'LL BE FIFTY-FIVE THIRTY-FOUR, SIR," the pretty young clerk at the grocery store says. Am I imagining the judgement in her tone? Or does she recognize me? After all, every week, I'm in here buyin' the same damn things.

Three cases of Shiner Bock, a couple frozen lasagnas, and a bag of cheddar cheese popcorn. I hate cooking and bein' at the stove for long periods ain't easy on my hip or leg. But I ain't bothered with a vegetable in months. If not longer.

The fine hairs on the back of my neck stand on end as the scents of jasmine and vanilla tickle my nose. Emi. She's only one register over, her phone pressed to her ear as she loads a handful of items onto the belt.

"Kyle, you don't have to explain. This story's blown up. I don't think the threats are serious, but you have a family. If you—or they—are even the slightest bit uncomfortable, you should move to midday until things blow over. I hate to lose you. Shit. I don't want to work with *anyone* else. But your wife and kids shouldn't be scared because of something *I* did."

I set the last case of beer in my cart. Emi's in full makeup, a light blue blouse, and a tight pencil skirt that barely reaches her knees. She still looks perfect, even at close to 9:00 p.m., and I catch myself before my stare heads into stalker territory.

Hold up. What threats?

I'm about ready to march over there and demand she explain when our gazes lock. The power behind her eyes—or maybe that's my dick remembering the quick kiss on the cheek she gave me the other night—makes me forget everything I was about to say.

A flash of green draws my attention. "Emi, your...err...parsley?...is about to fall off the belt."

Arching a brow, she snags the leafy bunch right before it loses its precarious balance and tumbles to the floor. "You mean the kale?"

"Kale?" Chuckling, I shake my head. "Ain't never heard of the stuff."

"Sorry, Kyle. I'm at the store." She gives me a shrug and mouths, "*Work thing,*" as she pulls a small bag of fruit from her basket.

She obviously didn't expect to see me here, and since she's still on the phone, I tip my Stetson to her. "Enjoy your night, Emi. I still hope you call me one of these days."

With her free hand, she traces an *X* over her heart with a smile. It's enough. For now.

"Gotta run, Kyle. But come see me tomorrow when you get in. We'll talk some more. And take advantage of the security Nelson offered, okay?" Ending the call, she meets the clerk's gave. "I'm sorry. Work emergency. Can I also get a book of stamps?"

"Sure, hon."

With one last glance at her small assortment of fruits and vegetables—along with a bag of the same cheddar cheese popcorn I favor—I head for my truck. I just made a fool of myself in front of a woman I'd love to take out on a date. How the hell was I supposed to know that was kale? Vegetables and I don't have much to say to one another.

I stow my groceries in the lockbox spanning the truck bed and run a hand through my hair. There's a reason I don't get out much

—or try to talk to women. And as much as I hope to hear from Emi soon, it's probably better if she loses my number permanently. She deserves someone who isn't so broken he can't even cook her a proper meal.

Something flickers in the corner of my right eye. Movement. Odd. I lost half the vision in that eye after the blast. Probably just a phantom. A misfire from my optic nerve. The doc said those were possible—likely even. But when it happens again, I turn.

A man in a black sweatshirt and dark Wranglers rises from the far side of Emi's powder-blue Mustang. His black ball cap is pulled low over his eyes. Something about the way he moves doesn't sit right with me, and I take two steps toward the car before he sprints away and disappears behind the back of the grocery store.

You spend long enough on the job, you start to trust your instincts as much or more than your eyes and ears, and my gut says that asshole was up to no good.

I can't let Emi drive away without checkin' out the whole damn car. And hearin' about the threats she mentioned.

Emi's heels click along the asphalt. A single bag is balanced on her hip. Her keys are already in her hand, held like a weapon. Not a very effective one. Most women—hell, even a lot of guys—don't have enough strength behind their punches to do serious damage with only a car key. But it's better than nothin'.

She clicks the key fob, and the car's lights flicker. But they're too dim. Something's very wrong.

"Emi?" I call as I take off at a run. "Wait."

A second later, the Mustang explodes with a *whoosh* of flames and enough force to drive us to the ground and slam Emi's head into the pavement.

MY EARS ARE RINGING like someone locked me in a bell tower, but everything else around me is muffled as fuck. Dragging my hand over my eyes, I wipe away a thick smear of blood. Emi is unnaturally still a few feet away. Crimson stains her cheek, and her whole face looks like she came down with a bad case of windburn. Or got dragged behind an angry bull.

I roll onto my side, a few deep breaths tamping down the dizziness.

Threats. She was being threatened. Someone named Nelson was offering security. Fuck me.

This wasn't an accident. That skinny sombitch in the black ball cap had something—or everything—to do with it. Flames crackle inside the wreckage, and a hubcap rattles at the far end of the parking lot as it rolls and finally hits a light pole.

"Emi?" Crawling as quickly as my aching leg allows, I make it to her side and check for a pulse. Thank God. She's alive. "Open your eyes, sweetheart." Her brows pinch together, and she tries to raise her head, but I press down on her shoulders. "Stay still."

"I...I can't...hear...what...?"

Leaning closer, I force strength into my tone. "Stay. Still. Someone blew up your car. Can you tell me what hurts?"

"My...car? Jasper?"

She's too confused to answer me properly, so I start a standard field assessment. The young clerk who rang up my groceries races out of the store and skids to a stop when she sees the burning car. "Oh my God. I'll call 911."

"Get an ambulance too!" I shout. "But don't say a *word* about who she is. You understand?"

"Huh?" The clerk clearly doesn't watch TV news. Too young. Probably sticks to the internet.

"Never mind. Call!"

Returning my focus to Emi, I shift my hold to her arms as she tries to sit up again. "Emmylou, keep still. That's an order."

"I'm not a soldier. You don't get to order me around." Slapping at my arms, she pushes up on an elbow. "Shit. The world isn't supposed to spin like that."

"I told you to stay down." I hate not being armed. That asshole could still be around. Watching to make sure he was successful. I have a concealed carry permit, but I was just going to the fucking grocery store.

My vision isn't totally clear. Vague shapes move at the other end of the parking lot—in the direction Baseball Cap guy headed. But one look at Emi and I know I can't leave her side. Not until the EMTs take a look at her. She lets me ease her back down to the ground, and thankfully, doesn't try to sit up again.

"Why are you here?" she asks, a wobble to her voice. "I keep running into you..."

"I was out shoppin'. Same as you. I only live a couple miles away. You're safe with me, sweetheart. I promise."

She blinks hard, then turns her head. Her eyes widen as she sees the still burning vehicle. "My car. Oh, God. My car's..."

"Replaceable. It might have been a pretty little thing, but it was *just* a thing. The ambulance is on its way. Cops too, I reckon. I'm gonna find your key fob. I want to see it before they take it into evidence. But you need to lie still, okay?"

I'm not sure she understands me. But she manages a little "uh-huh" and presses the heel of her hand to her forehead. Moving slowly, carefully, I search the few feet around us until I find the hunk of black plastic. Looks completely normal. No strange scratches or evidence anyone tampered with it.

The sirens are getting closer now, and I sink down onto my ass next to Emi. "So, you gonna tell me who's threatenin' you and why they want you dead?"

She rolls onto her side and curls inward. "It was probably an electrical fault." She doesn't sound convinced, but it's damn clear she doesn't want to talk to me about it.

"Whoa there. You could have a spinal cord injury. Or a concussion." Up close, her makeup half-blasted off by the explosion, she's so *real*. As real as the other night when we had dinner at the sports bar. But with one hundred percent more bruises bland scrapes. Her lips curve into a pout—or a grimace, I can't quite tell—when I try to get her to stay still.

"I don't have a spinal cord injury," she mutters and sits up. Then...fuck. Leans into me with her head against my bicep. "A concussion...that's a distinct possibility." After a moment, she sighs. "You were really here shopping. Beer and lasagna and... popcorn?"

"Yes, ma'am. Lucky I was, too. I think I saw someone messin' with your car before you came out of the store."

"Oh, God." She presses closer, and I wrap my arm around her slight shoulders. "I didn't think the threats were real...I have to call Nelson." Looking around, her eyes unfocused, she murmurs, "My purse...I have to find..."

I tighten my arm around her, keeping her where I know she's safe—tucked against my side. "I'll find it for you in a few minutes. As soon as the ambulance gets here."

Before she can protest, Austin PD and the EMTs arrive. It shouldn't feel so *wrong* to let the medics guide her to the ambulance while I tell one of the fresh-faced officers from the local precinct what happened, but it does.

"And you're sure this guy was messing with her car?" the officer —Devlin—asks. He can't be more than twenty-three, and I think this is the most excitement he's ever had on the job.

"Yes. Get a sketch artist out here and I'll give them a full description."

"Um, I don't think I'm authorized..." He turns to his partner, and the other guy shakes his head.

"Fuckin' hell. Look, I was a Ranger for more than a decade and Austin PD before that. I know it's not standard procedure. But I can ID the guy. Call your Sergeant. Tell him who I am and what I used to do for a living. He'll make it happen. Otherwise, he's hearing from me first thing in the mornin'."

"Yes, sir," Devlin says. "Sorry, sir."

"Don't call me sir. Just...make it happen. And send someone to the hospital to keep an eye on that woman. You hear me?" Glancing over at Emi sitting in the ambulance with a blanket around her shoulders, something stirs in my gut. I hardly know her. But while I held her...we shared something. A moment. A connection. One I don't want to end.

But it does, because the ambulance doors close and the vehicle whisks her away to Austin Memorial, leaving me alone with the last of the units on scene packing up.

"Sir?" Devlin clips his radio back in place as he approaches. "You can reach out to Detective Mitchell in the morning. The sketch artist went home a few hours ago."

Shit. Of course they did. It's almost 10:00 p.m.

"Will do. Thanks." What the fuck was I expecting? All hands on deck for what looks—to anyone who didn't see the guy in the baseball cap—like a bad car fire?

I should head to the hospital to check on Emi. The EMTs cleared me and I can't do shit here but watch as they load the remains of her car onto a tow truck for transport. So why am I leaning against my tailgate scanning the parking lot? Because my gut is screaming that the cops missed something.

As soon as the last patrol car leaves, I walk the perimeter, looking for anything out of place. A pair of footprints are clearly visible in mud at the far corner, and I pull out my phone and snap a couple of photos. Cops should have seen these, but even after they found out what I used to do for a living, they didn't give my theory about the guy in the black baseball cap much more than a passing nod. Fuckers.

I'm almost back to my truck when a bright red flash of color catches my eye next to the dumpster. Emi's purse—and her groceries. I should track down those two officers and give them a piece of my mind.

Don't get involved, Jasper. You'll find nothing but trouble. Bring Emi her purse, make sure she's okay, then go home.

We've shared a single meal and a few stolen moments. I shouldn't feel this much this soon. But my heart ain't about to listen to reason. So I spend a full five minutes retrieving her apples, yogurt, and kale before stowing the grocery bag in the lockbox and tucking her purse under my arm.

I'm going to the hospital and I'm not leaving until Emi tells me *exactly* what's going on.

CHAPTER EIGHT

Jasper

Austin Memorial is pure chaos. Unsurprising. It's almost 11:00 p.m., and the drunk drivers are out in force. Mix that with the standard bar fights and random acts of stupidity in a town this size, and I'm just a face in a crowd when I approach the Information Desk.

The frazzled young thing gives me a weak but friendly grin as I lean my hip against the counter. "I need to see a woman who came in by ambulance maybe forty-five minutes ago. Last name Marsh."

"I'm so sorry," she says, all warmth gone from her tone. "Unless you're family, I can't give you any information about a patient. Or even confirm if they're here. HIPAA regulations."

"Who's the charge nurse tonight?" I ask.

"Um..." Her blue eyes take me in, and the moment she realizes I know my way around hospital politics, she softens a fraction. "Luke Everett."

"Can you get him for me, please?"

Less than ten minutes later, I'm standing outside one of the curtained triage areas. Emi's voice carries over the chaos of the ER.

"I'm not staying here overnight. I'm *fine*."

"Ms. Marsh," a woman says, her tone patient—if not a bit patronizing, "if you want to leave against medical advice, there are a few forms we need you to fill out. But you have a mild concussion and it really would be better if you let us monitor you until morning—"

"I don't like hospitals. And I need a phone. I can't find mine. Or my purse. Shit," Emi says. The panicked edge to her voice worries me, but I don't know if she's decent. Barging in probably ain't smart. Then again, no one's ever accused me of brilliance.

Careful to pin my gaze no higher than the side of the bed, I step around the curtain, remove my hat, and hold Emi's purse at arm's length. "I can help with that last part."

"Jasper? Oh, my God. You brought my bag. Give it here." She throws back the blanket covering her legs, then grabs her left shoulder. "Dammit."

"Easy there." I set the scuffed bag next to her on the narrow bed. Her hospital gown rides up her thigh, revealing a nasty bruise —along with miles of smooth skin. "You hit the ground pretty hard, sweetheart."

Emi ain't paying me no never mind. She's too busy rummaging through her purse. With each passing second, relief eases more of the tension lines crinkling around her eyes. After she pulls out her tablet and checks the screen, she clutches it to her chest with a sigh. "I can't believe I left this behind. My entire *life* is on this thing."

Her long brown hair is mussed and tangled, half a leaf clinging to the strands. I slip it free, letting it flutter to the ground at my feet. "Well, it was hidden behind a dumpster. And that's a nasty bruise on your head. I have your groceries too. I reckon most of them survived. Even the kale."

Emi laughs, then winces as she presses a hand to her side. "Shit. That kind of hurts. But really...parsley? How could you confuse the two?"

"I don't cook much. You should let them keep you here overnight." I'm about to tell her she'll be safe here at the hospital —once I get a couple of Rangers stationed outside whatever room they put her in—when the nurse breezes back into the room.

"This handsome gentleman is right, you know," she says. "Concussions are serious business, darlin'."

"No. I...I can't." Emi grabs the clipboard from the nurse and scribbles her signature across the bottom of the page. "Hospitals... aren't for me. I need—I have to get out of here. N-now."

She's practically shaking. I reach for her hand, desperate to comfort her, to protect her, but she ignores me and scoots to the edge of the bed.

"Emi—" If someone did try to kill her tonight, home is the last place she should be going. But after giving me a look that could cut glass, she pushes to her feet. "Whoa, sweetheart. Don't turn around unless you want to give me a show."

Her side-eye is Oscar-worthy. "Don't watch unless you want one."

Holy shit. Emmylou Marsh might be the woman of my dreams. Smart, beautiful, and sassy as fuck. But she's also in trouble, and I can't let her leave here alone.

"I'll...uh...be right outside."

"I need five minutes, then I'll get those groceries from you and be on my way." She sways, her eyelids fluttering for a beat before she braces her hand on the bed and glares at me.

Well, that's a dismissal if I've ever heard one. Don't mean I won't try to change her mind. And convince her to go to a hotel, a friend's house, anywhere but home.

Emi

Maybe I should have asked the nurse to stick around. Getting dressed by myself is...harder than I expected. Every inch of my body is bruised and swollen. My heart won't stop racing, and I'm so close to a panic attack, it feels like I just got kicked in the chest.

I have to sit down on the bed to finish buttoning my blouse. I should be *better* by now. It's been twenty-four years. But the scar at my bikini line aches like it was yesterday.

Breathe. In and out. You're fine.

Except, I'm not. I have a concussion, my car is burnt to a crisp, and as of three hours ago, Eugene Fowler still hadn't been arrested. I don't know what the FBI is waiting for. After this evening's piece, they should have all the evidence they need to prove he's working with the cartel.

My head throbs with every beat of my heart. A burst of nausea crawls up my throat. Shit. That's bad. I need a hot shower and a good night's sleep. Tomorrow, I'll call Agent Van and demand an update.

Easing my purse strap over my shoulder, I sway on my feet for a moment until I get my bearings. I can't believe Jasper rescued my groceries too. What kind of guy *does* that?

My phone, still buried under my notebook, sunglasses, wallet, and lipstick, rings. I barely manage to answer before the call goes to voicemail. "Nelson, I'm fine," I say when my boss starts talking a mile a minute.

"I knew I shouldn't have let you leave without a bodyguard. You got another five death threats after your report aired tonight, Emi. This is *serious!*"

"Fowler didn't try to kill me," I protest. "People as *successful* as he is don't do this. He's an ass and he'll go to jail for a while, but he's loaded enough it'll be at some cushy country club facility with a gourmet chef and a certified yoga instructor on staff. He wouldn't risk an *actual* murder charge over a couple million in bribes."

"What if it's not a couple of million?" Nelson asks. "What if it's a hell of a lot more? Emi, just because this might be the world's most predictable *Law & Order* plotline doesn't mean it can't happen. To you."

I roll my eyes, then almost fall back on the bed from the motion. My headache intensifies, and while I'm no longer dizzy— or at least not *very* dizzy—I'm clearly not in great shape.

I *should* stay. I know that. But all I can think about is lying on a gurney bleeding out three days before Homecoming. If my mom and sister had come home ten minutes later, I would have died. Instead, I had a hysterectomy and started hormone replacement therapy at seventeen.

I have to get out of here. Right now.

Carefully, I pull back the curtain, step into the hall, and run right into Jasper. "Shit. Sorry."

"Emi? What's going on?" Nelson's voice rises until he sounds like a screeching demon spawn, and I cringe.

"Nothing. I'll see you tomorrow. But probably not until after noon. We can call the FBI together and tell them what happened. We can even talk about that bodyguard again."

He grumbles something that might be, "Okay," and ends the call.

In reality, nothing is even *close* to okay, but I'm too tired to fight with him tonight. All I want is a handful of ibuprofen and my bed.

Jasper shoots me a look I'm too exhausted to figure out. "Boyfriend?" he asks.

There's a smudge of dirt on his short beard, right at his chin. I reach up and brush it away, almost losing myself in his deep blue eyes. His hair is swept back from his face like he's been running his hand through it all night, and for the first time, I notice a few strands of gray at his temples.

Covering my hand with his, he holds me in place. "Emi? Did you hear me?"

Hear...? Shit. I'm so exhausted, I can't focus. What did he ask me? Oh, right. Boyfriend.

"No, sorry. Nelson's the news director at Channel 5." Three guys, all dressed in scrubs, race down the hall. I try to get out of the way, but I'm not steady on my feet—not in these heels—and pitch sideways into Jasper.

"Careful there, sweetheart." His strong arm wraps around my waist, and stars and garters. The expression—one my grandmother used to say all the time—just seems to fit with Jasper, though I'm not sure I've ever used it before in my life. He's so solid. And completely focused on me. "You really should stay at the hospital tonight."

"No. No, I can't." My heart starts to race. "I have to get out of here." My vision starts to tunnel, and my throat tightens. "P-please, Jasper. Let...go..."

"Do you trust me?" His voice rumbles through me, deep and sexy and full of that twang I've always associated with home. With safety.

Amid the chaos of the emergency room, I hang on to that feeling, despite my panic. He's so earnest. Like there's nothing he can't—or won't—do to keep me safe. Jasper Blade is as honest as they come.

I can't find my voice, but I nod. Carefully.

Jasper sighs. "I suppose that's good enough for now. I know a quick way out through cardiology."

With his arm still tight around my waist, he steers me through the halls. As soon as we pass through a set of double doors, it's quieter and calmer. The scent of blood starts to fade into the background. Two minutes later, we're outside, only a couple hundred feet from a big, hunter green pickup truck.

The lot isn't full. Not by a long shot, and a cool breeze prickles against my cheeks. Suddenly I'm very, *very* aware of how vulnerable I am. He was a Ranger. I *know* he's a good guy. But an hour ago, someone *blew up my car*.

"This...uh...thank you, Jasper. For everything. But I can manage from here. I'll call a rideshare to take me home." I duck out from under his arm, teetering on the uneven pavement for a moment before I can steady myself.

"Sweetheart, I ain't leavin' you out here. If you insist on calling that car, I'll wait with you until it shows up. But I'd much rather drive you home. Or...to a hotel. Or hell, to my place. Anywhere you won't be alone." Jasper guides me toward his truck with a hand at the small of my back, unlocks a storage box in the bed, and pulls out my bag of groceries. "What the hell *is* kale anyway? Fancy spinach? It looks like I should be feedin' it to a horse."

"It's *not*—" A wave of pain blooms across my forehead, and my stomach twists. "Shit."

Before I double over, Jasper's there, steadying me, letting me lean against him. "You're not staying by yourself tonight, Emi. You didn't much like the idea of coming home with me, so I'll give you three choices. Go back inside, go to a friend's, or let me sleep on your couch."

"I can't do any of those things." Taking a step away from him, I pull out my phone. "I'll be fine. I promise. My building is secure."

He huffs out a breath, setting the canvas grocery bag down next to me and shoving the kale back inside. The fire in his eyes should scare me, but instead, I feel safe. Protected. "Fine. But I'm waiting with you until the car shows up *and* you're giving me your number so I can check on you in a few hours."

"A town car will be here in seven minutes." I show him my screen, then sink down onto one of the benches along the side of the building. "You don't need to wait with me. There's a whole hospital full of people thirty feet away. It's been a terrible night, I barely know you, and I'd really like to be alone now."

Tears prick at my eyes, and I lean forward with my elbows on my knees. I'm being a bitch to him, and I don't know why.

Jasper takes a few steps back, removes his hat, and holds it over his heart. "I figure you could learn quite a bit about me if you wanted to. You bein' Channel 5's star reporter and all."

Despite my body feeling like an old punching bag, I start to laugh. Big mistake, as it makes the pounding in my head so much worse. "Star reporter? That's not a thing."

"It is from where I'm standin'. Your reporting on that Fowler asshole was damn fine work."

Leaning against the door of his truck, he crosses his legs at the ankles and shoves his hands into the pockets of his Wranglers. His eyes dart around the parking lot, lingering briefly on each shadow, each person heading to or from a car.

Shit. I haven't been paying attention to anything around me. What if Eugene Fowler *is* trying to kill me? What if he knows he didn't succeed at the grocery store? What if he found out which hospital I was taken to?

My phone screen isn't as clear as it was a few minutes ago. God.

I'm so tired. I want to sleep for a week, wake up, and find out this was all a bad dream.

The rideshare app buzzes. No. This can't be happening. The car's ten minutes away now and headed in the wrong direction. Another blink, and it's twelve minutes away. For the love of all that's holy in this world, I want to go home.

"Jasper?"

In two shakes, he's in front of me, crouching down with a grunt so we're almost eye level with one another. "You okay?"

I show him my phone screen. Fifteen minutes now. "I...could you...?"

"I'll drive you home, Emi." He holds out his hand, his fingers curling around mine to help me to my feet. "Thank you for trusting me."

"Seeing as you saved my kale..."

Jasper opens the passenger door and practically lifts me into the seat. "I just might have to try it one of these days."

CHAPTER NINE

Jasper

EMI DRIFTS off less than five minutes after giving me her address. Dammit if I don't want to drive around all night so I can keep stealing glances at her. But she has a bruise on her forehead the size of a golf ball, and her eyes are puffy.

She needs her own bed, a couple of ice packs, and someone watching over her until morning.

Her apartment building is one of Austin's nicest. As I pull into the parking lot, the speed bumps jolt her awake, and she whimpers softly.

"Easy now, sweetheart. Nothin's wrong. We're here."

"Oh." Her fingers flutter along the edge of the bruise on her forehead. "Shit. That isn't going to be pretty in the morning."

"I reckon you ain't gonna be on camera for a few days. At least, I hope not." If I could, I'd get her out of town, but I'm not even sure she'll let me stay with her tonight. I can't push her for more.

Get over yourself, Jas. You're in no shape to protect her. Not anymore.

"I have to finish the story," she whispers. "But...not tomorrow.

Need to sleep..." Her words are starting to slur, and she rests her head against the seat back.

"Fuckin' hell, Emi. You should have stayed at the hospital. What if that concussion turns into a brain bleed? I'm sleepin' on your couch tonight."

"No, you're not." She jerks up, her eyes unfocused, those big brown saucers rimmed with red. "You can help me out of this damn truck. Hell, I'll even let you walk me to my door. But that's *it*."

"We'll see about that," I mutter as I round the hood and pull open her door. She's already got one foot on the running board. With a concussion. In those heels. I need to touch her more than I need to breathe, and I mold my hands to her waist to ease her the rest of the way down.

Emi sways for a moment, giving me the perfect excuse to hold on. "Careful there. You ain't steady. Lean against the truck while I get your *kale*."

Her anger chills the air between us. Or maybe that's the late October night. She starts for the building's front door on her own, but before she can make it more than three steps, I'm at her side with her canvas grocery bag slung over my shoulder.

The building isn't too shabby. She punches in a six-digit code to enter the lobby, and there's a security guard sitting at the desk in front of the elevators. "Good evening, Ms. Marsh. You having a good night?" the man asks.

"I'm fine, Benny. Thanks for asking." Emi jabs the button for the elevator while the guard goes back to watching something on the monitor in front of him.

I scan the lobby. There's an electronic keypad on the stairwell door, and before we get onto the elevator, I catch sight of a pistol strapped to Benny's hip. The doors don't close until Emi enters another six-digit code on the security panel.

"Benny any good at his job?" I ask when we start to rise.

Emi braces a hand against the mirrored wall, fighting to keep her swollen lids at half mast. "If I hadn't said 'thanks for asking,' he would have called the police."

"You ain't serious…?"

She gives me the side eye. Fuck. She is.

"That's brilliant. He do that with all the residents?" I'm impressed, and that doesn't happen often.

"Yeah." She's slurring her words again, and I wrap my arm around her waist to keep her upright. "Jasper…I can manage—"

"You probably can. But if my mama found out I let you, she'd slap the taste outta my mouth. I'm well north of forty, but that wouldn't stop her from tryin'."

The elevator doors open on the sixth floor, revealing plush blue carpet lining the halls, and fancy etched glass lights every ten feet. I'm half expecting classical music to start pouring from hidden speakers any second.

Emi stops in front of Unit 608 and digs around in her purse until she comes up with her keys. But she misses the lock twice.

"Let me, sweetheart," I say as I ease the chain from her hand.

"I'm not an invalid." After a second, she sighs. "Shit. I'm sorry. This…isn't me."

I pull her against me again and press a kiss to the top of her head. "You're exhausted. Probably in a fair bit of pain too, I reckon. Come on. Let's get you into bed."

"I can find my own damn bed," she slurs.

"Sure. Just consider me a backup plan." The apartment is every bit as swanky as the lobby and the hall. Ain't much personal about it, though. Floor-to-ceiling windows look out over the glittering lights of downtown. Flipping a switch on the wall, I get my first good look at the living room. Three chairs, a coffee table, TV, and a deep purple area rug over the hardwood floor.

No couch. Guess I'm sleepin' on the floor tonight, because I sure as shit ain't leaving her alone. We lurch down the hall together, my hip on fire, and her eyes mostly closed.

Her bedroom is pristine. Not a single sock on the floor or wrinkle in her duvet.

"Sit down, sweetheart." She sinks onto the mattress, and as soon as I drop to one knee to remove her shoes, she tries to bat my hands away. "Emi, stop. I'm gonna take care of you tonight. In the mornin', you can kick me out and you never have to see me again."

"Want to see you again."

The whispered words send my dick pressing against the zipper of my Wranglers.

"Then maybe you'll let me take you on a proper date this weekend. If you feel up to it. But right now, you're goin' to sleep."

I *should* help her out of her clothes, but if I do that, I won't catch a wink tonight.

"I'll be out in the living room if you need anything." Pulling back the blankets, I lift her legs onto the bed. God, her skin is so soft. Long, lean muscles—she must be a runner—relax under my touch.

"Jasper," she murmurs. Her eyes are already closed, her hair fanned out on the blue satin pillow case. "S'no couch. Where...will you...?"

"The floor is just fine for me, sweetheart. I'm gonna wake you up around 2:00 a.m. Gotta make sure your concussion hasn't gotten any worse." Leaning down, I press a kiss to her forehead. I can still smell the smoke from the blast on her skin, but underneath, she's all jasmine and vanilla.

Despite being so tired my eyes feel like sandpaper, I take a few minutes to put away her groceries as best as I can. Gonna have to look up what to do with kale one of these days.

None of her chairs look big enough for a guy like me to catch some shuteye, so I grab a couple of throw pillows, kick off my boots, and stretch out on the floor next to the coffee table. It'll have to do. I set the alarm on my phone for 2:00 a.m., and say a quick prayer no one comes after Emi tonight.

Emi

Moving hurts. So does breathing. My head pounds an incessant beat any drummer would be proud of. Stretching, I feel the sheets whisper over my bare calves, but my underwire is digging into my side. Why am I in bed fully dressed?

It takes another few moments for my thoughts to start making even a lick of sense. My car caught fire. No. It exploded.

Fragments of memories hit me one after another. Riding in the ambulance. The way the hospital smelled—antiseptic and bleach and blood. Jasper showing up with my purse—and my groceries. The beginnings of a panic attack. Then him driving me home.

We were in the elevator together. Weren't we? But after that... everything's fuzzy.

The blinds are open, letting in the light from the full moon. It hurts my eyes. That can't be good.

"What if that concussion turns into a brain bleed? I'm sleepin' on your couch tonight."

Jasper. Did he really stay? Carefully, I push up on one elbow. So far so good. I'm only a little dizzy. Sitting all the way up is dicier, but after a minute, the room stops spinning.

I get to my feet in stages. Legs over the side of the bed. Hand braced on the headboard. Standing—I'm almost straight.

The stench of burnt gasoline clings to me. I'm not steady enough to shower, but I can at least get out of these clothes. And this damn push-up bra.

Everything takes twice as long as it should. Unbuttoning my blouse. Dealing with the zipper on my skirt. The catch on the bra is near impossible with how my fingers are shaking, but I finally get it off. Hallelujah.

I feel a hell of a lot better once I'm in my softest pajama pants and a t-shirt. A quick search of my bedroom doesn't turn up my purse—or my phone—so I make my way out into the living room.

Oh, my God. Jasper really did stay. He's stretched out on the floor next to the window with his Stetson angled over his eyes. At least he grabbed one of the chair cushions for under his head.

Carefully, I sink down to my knees next to him. "Jas?" I gently nudge his shoulder. "Jasper? Wake up."

He jerks to sitting, his hat tumbling to the carpet, and wraps his hands around my upper arms. "Emi? What's wrong?"

"I'm fine." It's such an absurd thing to say, I start to laugh until a sharp pain lances through my skull. I hiss out a breath, and Jasper arches his dark brows at me. "Okay. I'm as fine as someone can be after...what happened."

"Then why are you up? Don't even *think* about trying to kick me out. I'm staying put." His confusion is honestly adorable.

I offer him a wobbly smile. "You can't sleep on the floor all night."

"If you had a couch, I wouldn't be down here."

"I live alone. What do I need a couch for? Besides, any couch big enough for you to sleep on wouldn't fit in this apartment." My thoughts are fracturing in real time, and if I don't lie down again soon, I'm probably going to fall over. "Come on. My bed is big enough for both of us."

"I'm fine out here," he says, but the longing in his voice is hard to miss. "I won't do anythin' that makes you uncomfortable."

"What makes me uncomfortable is thinking of you out here on the floor." I try to get up, but my body decides now is a good time for me to lose all sense of equilibrium. I pitch forward, landing sprawled across a set of powerful legs with my ass in the air.

Well, this is a great look.

"Emi, fucking hell. I'm taking you back to the hospital." Jasper pulls me into his arms, brushing my hair away from my face. The concern in his blue eyes is something I should have been prepared for. But the intensity of it sends a ball of heat churning in my belly.

"No." The heat turns to ice in a heartbeat. There's no way I'd survive a whole *night*—even half of one—in the hospital. "I have a headache. I'm sore. But I'm *fine*. If you care about me getting any rest at all, you'll...you'll find my phone so I can plug it in, then come sleep in my room."

He must understand just how *not* on board I am with any talk about going back to the hospital, because he sighs. "Don't suppose I'd get very far anyway. Benny would ask how you're doin', you wouldn't give him the code word, and he'd have my ass arrested. That sound about right?"

I almost laugh again, but I remember how well that worked

out for me the last time, so I try for a sweet smile instead. "You were a highly decorated Ranger, Jasper. You wouldn't spend more than a few hours in lockup."

"Fuck me." He shifts me gently off his lap and onto one of the chairs. "I'd never hear the end of it either."

"Then get up. I'm exhausted, and I won't sleep knowing you're out here on the floor." In truth, I'll pass out the second I close my eyes, but Jasper doesn't need to know that. "Oh, and I need my phone or it'll be dead by morning. Where did you put my purse?"

Jasper lumbers to his feet with a groan. Lines of pain tighten around his lips. He limps over to my small table, retrieves my bag, and sets it next to me. "How bad's the headache? Scale of one to ten?"

"Three." That's a bald-faced lie, but with my head bent rummaging through my purse, hopefully he won't notice my flushed cheeks. Five or six would be closer to the truth. My fingers close around my phone, and I check the screen, but it's too blurry for me to see much of anything. Shit. That's probably not a good sign.

"Emi, look at me." The command in his tone is impossible to ignore. His eyes are bloodshot, and there's a small cut over his left brow. "Follow my finger."

I'd roll my eyes if I weren't afraid I'd pitch over from the motion. So I do what he asks. After I've recited the days of the week—backwards—told him what I ordered when we met at the sports bar, and confirmed my ears weren't ringing, he holds out his hand.

"Back to bed with you." I should refuse his help, but tucked against his side, I feel safe in a way I haven't since the Fowler story first hit the air. When he tries to tuck me in, though, I point to the other side of the bed.

"You're not the only one whose mama raised them to be hospitable. I don't have anything big enough to fit you, but as long as you're not going commando, you don't need to sleep in your jeans or t-shirt. We're both adults."

I sink back against the pillows and stifle a yawn. Jasper sheds his jeans and t-shirt. Damn. In only a pair of black boxer briefs, he's sexy as hell. Too bad I'm so tired I could cry.

Once he's under the covers, I let myself relax. But despite how exhausted I am, sleep doesn't steal me away. I try a couple different positions, but each one aggravates one bruise or another.

"Emi, if you don't stop wrigglin', I'm gonna have a problem I can't do nothin' about," Jasper manages when my ass brushes his hip.

"Sorry. I didn't realize how banged up I was." Curling on my side facing him, I shove a hand under my pillow. "Or how big you were, apparently."

He chuckles. "I'll go back out to the living room—"

"No. Stay." I snag his arm, his skin so warm against my fingers. "Please."

"On one condition." He turns so he can study me in the semi-darkness. "You tell me why you hate hospitals so much that you'd check out against medical advice."

Of course, he'd ask me about the one thing I don't share with *anybody*. I could deflect. I *should* tell him I'm tired and we'll talk in the morning. But he could have been seriously hurt tonight because of me. I won't lie to him again.

"When I was seventeen, I started feeling...weird. Nauseous and exhausted all the time. My periods were really irregular, and my boyfriend and I had only done it once, so I didn't even think..." He stiffens, and I worry this is a *very* bad idea. But I'm committed now. "I was a little over three months along when I started bleeding."

Jasper doesn't say a word, thank God, but he does cover my hand with his.

"I didn't tell anyone for two days. But by then, I was in so much pain, I couldn't hide it anymore. My mother took me to the doctor. He was old school. You know the type—small town, family values..." A bone-weary sigh parts my lips. "He said I needed to let nature take its course." My voice wobbles. I twine my fingers with Jasper's and hold on tight. "I stayed home from school the next day. I don't remember much, but my mom found me unconscious around four. Uterine hemorrhage. Sepsis. They had to..." Tears well in my eyes, trailing across my nose and down my temple. "I spent a week hooked up to so many machines, I could barely move. And seventeen is way too young for a hysterectomy."

"Fuck, sweetheart." Jasper scoots closer, and I can't help it. I let him put his arms around me and rest my head on his chest. "What do you need? Right now."

"Just...hold me," I whisper, suddenly so tired, I can barely get the words out.

"Yes, ma'am." He shifts slightly, and one hand strokes gently up and down my back. "I'm right here. And I'm not going anywhere."

Maybe it's the warmth of his touch, or sharing my deepest secret, but the tension drains from my body by degrees. "That's why I couldn't stay in the hospital." The words slip over my tongue before I can stop them.

My throat burns with unshed tears, the way it always does when I think about what could've been. It's not that I have a strong desire to have kids, but knowing the choice was taken from me... *that* was a violation. A crime. A tragedy.

For a long moment, Jasper is still, and I wonder if I've said too much. Or maybe he thinks I'm *less* now that he knows the truth. Less of a woman. Less of a person. Not worth his time.

Stop it.

I make a move to wriggle free, but he tightens his grip. "I'm so fucking sorry, Emi."

The emotion in his tone tells me everything he can't say. Because there are no words. Not for this.

My eyes, flutter shut, and a tear splashes my cheek, following the invisible path etched onto my skin from years of mourning this pain. "Me too."

CHAPTER TEN

Jasper

THE FIRST RAYS of the morning sun hit my face. Fuck. Emi is wrapped in my arms with her head tucked under my chin. She barely stirred all night, but I couldn't sleep a wink. Not with her warm, soft body pressed up against me.

I laid awake for hours watching her. She was too damn young to go through something like that. Too damn innocent.

And so fucking brave to share her pain with me.

If I don't move—and soon—she'll wake up with my dick pressed up against her ass, and I'll catch hell for it. I've seen several sides of Emmylou Marsh the past week. Determined. Polished. Excited. Even a little scared. But angry? I'm not sure I'd survive angry.

Carefully, I ease her onto her back. The bruise over her left eye looks ten times worse this morning. Dammit. I should have insisted she put some ice on it last night. Half a dozen small scratches mar her cheeks and forehead. If she'd been any closer to the car, she could have been seriously hurt. Or worse.

Tugging on my Wranglers and t-shirt, I shuffle out into Emi's living room. My phone battery is down to ten percent, but that should be enough to get some information out of my brother.

Jasper: Car bomb went off at the Ninth and Molder Stop-N-Shop last night at 9:17 p.m. I need you to look into the case. I think someone tried to kill Emmylou Marsh.

AJ better not blow me off. I know he's going through an ocean of shit, but he's still a goddamned Ranger.

I stare at Emi's fancy coffee machine for five full minutes. There are so many buttons, I'm afraid I'll somehow launch a nuke if I'm not careful. But fuck, I need caffeine.

My phone buzzes on the counter before I find a mug.

AJ: The case is with Austin PD. Give me one good reason why I should call in a chit for this.

Jasper: Because I asked you to, asshole. And because I doubt Officer Devlin's been out of the academy more than a month.

AJ: Give me an hour. I haven't even had my coffee yet.

That makes two of us. I've gotta figure out how this damn machine works. It's either that or sneak out before Emi wakes up. But if I did that, I couldn't lock her door. Even with Benny downstairs—if he's still on shift—I can't take that chance.

Five tries—and one mess of spilled coffee later—I have a cup. The jolt fuels me enough, I find a travel mug in Emi's cabinet and fumble my way through making what I *think* is an almond milk cappuccino.

Careful not to spill either cup, I shuffle down the hall and back into her bedroom. She's still asleep. Easing my hip onto the edge of the mattress, I brush her hair away from her face. "Emi? Sweetheart I need you to wake up for me."

She groans, her eyes opening to slits. "What time is it?"

"A little after eight. Do you know where you are?"

That riles her enough to glare at me. "Of course I know where I am. I told you last night—err, this morning—I was fine." Her nose wrinkles, and suddenly, she's not angry anymore. "You made coffee."

As if she's only now seeing the mug in my hand, she sits up and reaches for it.

"This one's mine," I say with a chuckle and pass her the travel mug. "But I made you a cappuccino. I think."

Her eyelids flutter with her first sip. "God, I would not make it in this world without coffee."

"Is it okay?" I ask. "Your machine is...somethin'."

Emi snorts, and the sound is so light, feminine, and *real*, my heart jumps in my chest.

"Best money I've ever spent," she says and takes another sip from the travel mug. Then her eyes narrow. "It's all push button. Did you have trouble with it?"

"Uh..." Fire licks up the back of my neck. "No. Not...much."

"Jasper!" She laughs but winces a moment later. "Shit. That hurts."

Instantly on alert, I take the mug from her and set it on the nightstand. "Tell me."

"Stand down, Ranger. I'm sore. Everywhere. But I'll be okay." She stares pointedly at me—at where I'm sitting on the edge of her bed. "I need my phone. Nelson is probably having a coronary. I should have texted him when we got here last night. Mind moving so I can get it off the dresser?"

"You stay right there. I'll get it for you."

Emi bristles at the command in my tone but then huffs and picks up the travel mug again. "Fine. But I'm not an invalid, Jasper. You took care of me last night and made me coffee this morning. I can handle things from here."

"We'll see about that," I mutter once I've handed her the phone. "I texted AJ a bit ago. I'm waitin' to see what he finds out from Austin PD. Until I can guarantee your safety, I ain't leaving."

With her phone in her hand, Emi snaps her gaze to mine. "Oh, *hell* no. I'm an adult. I can get myself to Channel 5. I appreciate everything you've done for me, but it's time for you to go."

Emi throws back the blanket, gets to her feet, and sways. She only makes it two steps in my direction before one of her knees buckles. I haul her against me, and she melts into my embrace.

"I'm not going anywhere, sweetheart. Not until we know there's no one after you. And *definitely* not with you falling over like that." I smooth a hand along her shoulder, and let it come to rest at the small of her back. She's so fucking beautiful, even with her hair mussed from sleep and that damn purple bruise on her forehead.

Emi tips her head back to meet my gaze. The need in her eyes sends all the blood shooting straight to my dick. These Wranglers are unbearably tight, and if she looks down, she'll see how much I want her.

"Jasper," she whispers. "I'm..."

I take a chance and press my lips to hers. She doesn't protest. A little moan vibrates in her chest. If she keeps that up, I'll come in my pants like a fucking teenager.

Stroking my tongue along the seam of her mouth, I beg her to open for me, and she does. Oh, God. She tastes of coffee, smells like jasmine, and feels so very right in my arms.

My phone vibrates in my front pocket, and the sensation forces us apart. I should ignore it. But...what if it's AJ?

Emi's cheeks turn a bright shade of crimson, and she wriggles out of my embrace. "I...need to shower. And charge my phone. And...um...brush my teeth."

I cover my mouth with my hand. Shit. I didn't even think about morning breath. My phone buzzes again. "I'll be out in the living room. If you feel dizzy at all, you call for me. No tryin' to manage on your own, you hear?"

After a huff, she nods. "Fine. But once you talk to your brother, you need to go home."

I shut her bedroom door with a quiet click and mutter under my breath, "We'll see about that."

Emi

I lean my back against the door. My cheeks are on fire. Jasper is a fantastic kisser. And he's in my living room. With a hard-on. I couldn't ignore the bulge in his jeans as he held me. And if it weren't for his over-the-top protectiveness, I probably wouldn't have made it home from the hospital.

I could march right out into the living room and demand he kiss me again. I would, if I weren't on the biggest story of my career. Or if I hadn't made a fool of myself at 2:00 a.m. telling him about the time I almost died. My hand flutters over my stomach, skimming the scar I'll bear for the rest of my life. I made my peace with what happened. Having kids was never in my plan—even as a teenager. But Jasper probably wants them.

Stop it. He kissed you, remember? After you told him everything. And he's still here.

I don't know what this is between us—other than a kiss that set me on fire and his obsession with keeping me safe—but I can't dwell on it now. In my addled state last night, I set my phone *next to* the charging pad rather than *on* it, so the damn thing is deader than dead. After I make sure it's charging, I sneak into the bathroom.

At least in here, I can lock the door and engage in the time-honored tradition of overthinking everything in the shower. Fowler, my burned-out car, Jasper, that kiss, my future...

The hot water feels like heaven cascading down my back. Until I try to run my fingers through my hair. I find at least three separate bruises on my head, and see stars every time I hit one of them untangling my unruly locks.

By the time I wrap myself in a towel and tiptoe back to my bedroom, though, I feel almost human again.

My usual wardrobe isn't going to cut it today, so I opt for a pair of black yoga pants and my favorite purple sweater. My face, however, is a lost cause. There isn't enough makeup in the whole country to hide the bruises, scrapes, and dark circles under my eyes.

My phone buzzes on the charger. Snagging it, I sink down onto my bed. Shit. Thirty-seven missed text messages and six calls—all with voicemail.

This can't be good. Four of the calls are from Nelson. Those can wait. The other two...a Detective Mitchell from Austin PD.

Glancing over at the closed door, I wonder if I should get Jasper. He'll want to listen in. Except...if there's even a shred of evidence someone purposely blew up my car, he'll never let me out of his sight again. And probably demand I go into hiding.

I press play on the first message.

"Ms. Marsh, this is Detective Nolan Mitchell with the Austin Police Department. You spoke to my colleague, Officer Devlin, last night after your car exploded. I'd like you to come into the station this morning so we can give you an update. Please call me at your earliest convenience."

Well, if that isn't the vaguest message in the history of vague messages. The second is no better. If anything, it's worse.

I try calling the detective back, but it goes to voicemail, and Nelson texts me *again* before the greeting finishes playing. This day is getting on my last nerve and it's only just started. If I don't respond, I'm afraid he'll send out a search party—or at least that bodyguard he keeps talking about.

Emi: I'll be in a little after noon today. I'm fine. Just sore. Once I talk to the police, I'll know if I need five minutes in the A block tonight.

Nelson: Five minutes? I thought your piece on Fowler was done for the week.

Emi: I thought so too. Until my car blew up. You wanted me to take the death threats seriously. Now, I might have to. I'll see you after lunch.

I hope Nelson understands that's my way of telling him to stop texting me every ten minutes. My head hurts too much to handle him when he's this *intense.*

Because now, I need to deal with someone who makes Nelson look like the chillest man on the planet.

Jasper.

CHAPTER ELEVEN

Emi

JASPER SITS at my breakfast bar, frowning at his phone, with a fresh cup of coffee at his elbow.

"Is everything all right?" I tug at my sweater, one of my many bruises protesting against my bra strap.

"My brother needs a permanent attitude adjustment," he mutters. "AJ made some calls to his contact at Austin PD. Have you heard from a Detective Mitchell?"

"He called twice this morning." I show Jasper the transcripts from the voice mail messages.

"That fucking idiot should know better than to leave such a useless goddamn message. That ain't much more than I got from AJ. Sombitches. Both of them."

I lean against the counter next to him. "Tell me how you really feel."

Jasper laughs, a rich sound that vibrates his entire being. I could fall for that laugh. Easily. Hell, I'm already falling for it—and him.

"Mitchell and my brother would probably get along like two

pigs in slop." He runs a hand through his hair, tugging on the dark brown strands. "You call him back?"

"I tried. But I might as well just go in. It'll be faster." I move to the fridge, rummaging inside for a container of yogurt. "Wait. You put my groceries away?"

"Yes, ma'am. Might have eaten some of your cheddar cheese popcorn, though. I missed dinner last night and left *my* groceries in the truck." He nods toward his hat and keys resting on the counter. "Whenever you're ready, I'll drive you to the station."

"You will do no such thing. For fuck's sake, Jasper. You have a life to get back to. I'm *fine*."

"I'm not askin'."

Well, *hello*. Over-the-top Jasper is sexy as hell. Even if I *do* want to give him a piece of my mind. "I'm a grown-ass woman, Jasper Blade. You don't get to tell me what to do."

He growls—actually *growls*—and it does something to me I'm not prepared for. I'll need to change my panties if he keeps this up. But I won't back down either. He does not get to tell me what to do and expect me to be happy about it. I ball my hands into fists at my sides so I'm not tempted to grab him and kiss him senseless.

"If you want to drive me, you can ask. Nicely. Maybe I'll say yes."

A vein in Jasper's temple throbs. To his credit, he only blows out a breath and closes his eyes for a beat. "Emi, will you please let me drive you to Austin PD?"

"Why, yes. I would love a ride since my car isn't...operational at the moment." I offer him a sweet smile, then pop the top of the container of yogurt. "Want some?"

He wrinkles his nose. "Got anything that ain't healthy?"

Now it's my turn to laugh. "Besides the cheddar cheese popcorn? Not at the moment. There's oatmeal? Or smoothie ingredients in the freezer?"

"Waffles, pancakes, muffins..." he says, longing in his tone.

"I'm in front of a camera anywhere from three to five nights a week. I rarely have time to cook, and broadcast news requires me to maintain certain physical...*standards*. Every couple of weeks, I splurge on the enchilada plate at Bar Roma. The rest of the time, it's yogurt, kale, and two handfuls of popcorn a night."

His blue eyes darken. "I'd say that's no way to live, but my standard grocery order is two boxes of frozen lasagna and a couple of cases of Shiner. So I guess I'm not in any position to judge."

"You're right. You're not." I only make it through half the yogurt before my stomach twists into a knot. "I'll be ready to go in five minutes."

Jasper

Emi is glued to her phone on the drive to Austin PD, but between text messages, she steals glances at me.

I can't read her. She doesn't think she needs a bodyguard, but she's got one—at least until I hear the bomb squad's report on her car. AJ was less than helpful when he finally called me back this morning.

"The detective on her case is Nolan Mitchell. He's an ass. But he's a decent detective with a high close rate. He wouldn't tell me anything, but he did let it slip that he'd gotten a call from the FBI."

If the FBI's involved, the explosion wasn't an accident. Emi *was* targeted. But did they want to kill her or merely scare her off the story?

I ease the truck into the parking spot with the best visibility in the lot. It's a police station, but that doesn't mean I'm taking any chances with Emi's safety. No one's sneaking up on us.

She throws her door open, but I reach across the cab to take her hand. "Wait for me to come around, sweetheart."

Goddammit. Why can't I stop with the "sweetheart" shit? Emmylou Marsh is not my girlfriend. Hell, she's barely a friend if the glare she's giving me is any indication.

"Are you always this overprotective?" she asks when I wrap my hands around her waist to help her down.

"Yes. No. Fuck. I don't know. I haven't spent a lot of time around people since the explosion." Scanning the lot, I note the half dozen cars, the mom pushing a stroller on the sidewalk, the clouds gathering on the horizon. Tonight's storm is gonna be a toad strangler.

"Why not?" She lets me keep my palm at the small of her back all the way to the station's front doors. "You're a nice guy, Jasper. Handsome too. Any woman would be lucky to snap you up."

A hint of sadness lingers in her tone. I don't have time to figure out why before she marches up to the information desk and asks to talk to Detective Mitchell.

I *should* offer to sit in the lobby until she's done. Instead, I reach for her hand. "I'm goin' in with you."

Emi's brow wings up. "Why am I not surprised? Fine. But if you try to talk over me even once, we're done. I get enough of that at work."

"I wouldn't dare try." Holding my Stetson to my heart, I wait for her to turn those big brown eyes to mine. "Emi, I'm not stayin' with you because I think you're weak. And it damn well ain't because you're a woman. I'm here because I care."

Her gaze softens. Does she squeeze my hand a little?

"Ms. Marsh?" An older man—late fifties if I had to guess— lumbers out from behind the security glass. His detective badge is clipped to his belt. From the way his jacket hangs, he's tucked his gun into his shoulder harness. "I'm Detective Mitchell. If you follow me, we can talk in one of the conference rooms."

Mitchell doesn't even toss a glance in my direction until Emi clears her throat. "This is Jasper Blade, detective. He's with me."

"We really should speak privately, Ms. Marsh," Mitchell says.

As if she knows I'm about to give the man a piece of my mind, Emi wraps her hand around my elbow and squeezes gently. "I trust Jasper. He was a Ranger until he retired last year, and he's...a friend." With a sweet smile, she adds, "I'm going to tell him everything less than five minutes after I walk out of here, Detective. Save me the trouble?"

The look Mitchell gives me could melt the polar ice caps. Yeah. He knows who I am. And he's not happy I'm here.

We follow him through the bullpen, down a hall, and into a

conference room. "Wait here," the detective says, then shuts the door with enough force to rattle the windows.

"What crawled up his ass?" Emi whispers.

"Ain't no love lost between Austin PD and the Ranger Division. They think we're cowboys who don't play by the rules."

She smirks, her brow arching in the cutest way. "And what do *you* think of *them*?"

Mitchell stalks back into the room, and I give Emi a quick wink. "One of these days, I'll tell you."

Sinking into a chair across from us, the detective flips open a folder. He spreads half a dozen photographs out on the table. The remains of Emi's car, some burned wires, and a blasting cap. "So, Ms. Marsh. Do you have any idea who might want to kill you?"

CHAPTER TWELVE

Emi

I HOLD it together until we're back in Jasper's truck. But once he starts the engine, I stare out the window while Detective Mitchell's words play on a loop in my head.

"We found the remains of a cell phone detonator. The techs estimate a quarter pound of C4 under your right wheel well—close enough to the gas tank, it was guaranteed to burn."

"Emi? Talk to me." At a stop sign, Jasper reaches over to rest his hand on mine. The warmth of his touch grounds me, though it doesn't make it any easier to find my voice.

"I thought for sure it was an accident," I say softly. "But someone really did try to kill me."

Jasper squeezes my fingers once, then returns his hand to the wheel. "Fowler won't get away with this, sweetheart. Mitchell might not have much to go on, and he's a colossal ass, but he has a respectable close rate."

"We don't even know that it *is* Fowler." I stifle a snort. "Ignore me. Of course it's Fowler. Or someone he's connected to."

"Do you always go to the grocery store on Thursday nights?" Jasper asks. "Or right from the station?"

"How did you know I'd come from work?"

He chuckles. "You were dressed to the nines, perfect makeup, heels…"

Oh. Right.

My cheeks heat, and I fiddle with the hem of my sweater to give myself something to focus on. "Saturdays. I normally shop on Saturdays."

The trees pass by in a blur of green and brown. Why do I suddenly feel like my whole life is nothing but a blur? I work all the time. Mama died when I was twenty-three. Every year, my sister asks me to visit her in London for her birthday, but there's always been a story. Or at least that's what I've told myself.

What if I never get the chance to see her again? I don't remember my life flashing before my eyes last night, but if it had, would I have seen anything but work?

"Emi?" Jasper brushes his hand along my arm. "We're here."

I jerk away from him, but the seatbelt traps me with nowhere to go. "What happens now?"

"I'm gonna walk you inside and make sure you're safe. Your boss hired bodyguards, right?" he asks.

"Y-yes. The building is secure, but he stationed two rent-a-cops in the lobby. My cameraman, Kyle, has a family. He was okay with a bodyguard following him home at night. I wasn't."

"Dammit, Emi. These guys aren't playing around. If you had been two steps closer to that car—"

"I know!" Tears well in my eyes. "I've worked in network news for almost twenty years. Death threats have always been part of the job. They never bothered me before. But they were never so *real* before either."

"They're real now, sweetheart." Jasper cups my cheek and skates his thumb gently below the bruising. "Once you're inside, I gotta go see my brother and slap some sense into him. But I'm only leavin' if you promise me you won't go anywhere alone."

"I'm not taking one of Nelson's bodyguards to the bathroom with me," I say with a gentle shake of my head. "I draw the line there."

Jasper laughs, the sound so rich and almost happy. "Good. But, I'm serious, Emi. You don't leave the station. Not for lunch, drinks, a walk...nothin'. I'll be back at seven."

"You don't need to babysit me," I bristle.

"Yes, ma'am. I do. Hell, I'd stay with you all day if you'd let me. But I reckon you've had about enough of my overprotective ass for a few hours. So you stay inside while I do what I've gotta to, and when I come back at seven, I'd like to take you to dinner. If that's okay with you."

I pull my hands away. "Jasper Blade, are you *flirting* with me?"

"No ma'am. I'm tryin' to ask you out on a proper date. Somewhere quiet, easily secured. Maybe even a little romantic. After that, we'll see what comes next."

Jasper scoots closer so only the center console separates us, slides his hand into my hair, and cups the back of my head. His kiss sends goosebumps racing along my arms, down my back, and all the way to my toes. Strong fingers gently caress the column of my throat. I moan into the touch.

His lips follow the curve of my jaw until he finds the shell of my ear. "I want you, Emmylou Marsh. Sleeping next to you last night—who am I kiddin', I was countin' stars the whole time."

I shudder. Jasper toys with the top button on my blouse. Shit. Anyone could walk by and see us... "Stop," I whisper. "Not...here."

He pulls back by inches. First his lips. Then his hands. Then his bulk and heat.

My breath stutters in my chest. I'm so damn needy, I'm tempted to suggest we find a hotel. Or go back to my place. But then I remember the photos of my mangled car. Of the remains of the cell phone that set off the bomb. I have work to do.

"Tonight. Okay. A...date," I manage. "At seven."

Jasper reaches over and cups my cheek. "I need to hear you say it, Emi. You won't go anywhere alone."

I want to rail against his demand. To tell him I'm not a child and I can protect myself. But I don't. Because he's right. I'm in trouble, and I need to be careful.

"I'll stay inside." I cover his hand with mine. "I promise."

Jasper

This day has been goin' downhill ever since I got out of Emi's bed this morning. I shoulda' stayed there. Made *her* stay with me. Then we might be able to pretend everything's normal. That no one's out to kill her.

Instead, I'm checking every corner of the Channel 5 lobby. Their security ain't half bad. No one gets past the front doors without badging in. A uniformed attendant monitors the reception desk, and from the way he carries himself, he's former military.

"You've walked me right to the door," Emi says, a little of the sass back in her tone. "No one would be stupid enough to come after me here. There's always a camera on somewhere in this building."

I don't like leaving her. But we aren't a couple. And she's right. If the cartel *is* involved, there's no fucking way they'd attack the station. No. They'd go after her and her alone. Make it look like an accident. Because that's plausible deniability.

"I'll be right back here at 7:00 p.m. When you hear from the FBI, you give me a call." Leaning in, I brush my lips to her forehead. "You might be the most interesting woman I've ever met, Ms. Marsh. Stay safe today. I want to see what this is between us."

With a smile, she walks backward all the way to the security doors. "So do I."

***

"He's not here, Jasper." Sergeant Parker Elmore rounds her desk, her blond hair swinging in a high pony tail.

"Then where is he? The sombitch was supposed to call me back two hours ago." The bullpen is mostly quiet this time of the afternoon on a Friday. Billings and McGrath are already gone.

Parker's surrounded by paperwork, which means my brother dumped it all on her before he took off.

Her blue and gold eyes darken. "The same place he is every Friday."

Fucking hell. "I thought he'd rented that apartment to *live* in. Not as his weeknight crash pad."

Parker rests her hip on the edge of AJ's desk and rubs the back of her neck. "He'll never give up the house, Jas. You know that. It's his last connection to Grace."

She's right. The place on Lake Travis was their dream home. Floor to ceiling windows, a fully outfitted custom outdoor kitchen, fire pit, an insulated man cave for AJ, and an art studio for Grace with a water view.

He stayed there for a year after she went missing in case she found her way home, but Billings and McGrath—two of his lieutenants—finally convinced him that living in that big house all alone wasn't good for him.

"I'll head out there next. But...I don't suppose you know anything about Detective Nolan Mitchell over at Austin PD, do you?"

"Nope," she says. "But I'll put some feelers out—*if* you do something for me."

"What?"

Parker's no fool. She's only been on the job for two years, but she's got the best instincts of anyone I know besides my brother—and maybe me.

"Go see him. He won't admit it, but he's really struggling, Jasper. Every Saturday he goes out on the same trail Grace used the day she disappeared. I know you can't run anymore, but maybe one day...you could go with him."

Fuck. I didn't know it was that bad. "I'll talk to him. Don't expect much. Big brother doesn't give two shits about what I have to say. But...I'll try."

DARK CLOUDS GATHER on the horizon as I park my truck next to AJ's black SUV. His lake-front property has seen better days. Brown patches of dead grass dot the front lawn, the bushes are so overgrown, they've started to block the windows, and his gutters are chock full of weeds.

The doorbell echoes through the house, but he doesn't answer. I give it one more try—and a good two minutes—before I head for the side gate. He used to keep a spare key under one of the planters by the back door.

Behind the house, the late afternoon sun hits the water. A stiff breeze turns the lake into a sea of glittering diamonds. I always loved this view. Hell, we'd sit out here for hours on a Saturday night with the fire pit going—back when AJ and Grace used to invite me over on the regular.

Belle, an Australian Shepherd/Bernese Mountain Dog mix, trots over to me and nudges my hand with her nose. The pup was so bonded to Grace that AJ had to give her anxiety meds for months. Belle didn't want to be anywhere but at the front door waiting for her person to come home.

"Wasn't sure you'd remember me," I say as I scratch Belle behind her ears. "But you're a smart girl." I squint up at the house, and though the sun against the tall windows threatens to blind me, I can make out AJ sitting in one of the Adirondack chairs on the deck. "Come on. Maybe he's got a tennis ball up there."

The dog sticks close to my side until I find an old, faded ball next to the steps. Then she starts dancing around me until I throw the mangled thing halfway to the lake.

"What are you doing here?" AJ asks, his gaze pinned to the water. A bottle of Shiner sits at his elbow.

"Thought I'd drop off a dictionary to remind you what the words, 'Give me two hours,' mean. You were supposed to call me back, asshole." I lower myself down into the chair next to him with a quiet grunt.

"Leg?" AJ sits up a little straighter, but he still doesn't look at me.

"And hip. The explosion knocked me on my ass last night." I

dig my knuckles into my thigh, but the pressure doesn't bring much relief. Only an ice pack and a couple bottles of beer can take the edge off.

Belle drops the tennis ball at my feet, her tongue lolling out of her mouth and her butt wiggling so fast it's practically a blur. AJ swipes it up before I can move. "No offense, Jas, but your pitching arm ain't worth shit anymore."

He's not wrong. The ball travels almost twice as far this time. Belle takes off like a shot. That dog can go for miles without getting the least bit worn out. Grace used to take her on long runs every weekend. If Belle had been with Grace that day...maybe she'd still be here. But she'd stepped on a wasp the day before, so Grace left her at home.

"Are you investigating Eugene Fowler?" I'm done mincing words with my brother. He's gonna give me a straight answer or I'm gonna kick his ass.

"Of course not!" He turns his head to meet my gaze. "For fuck's sake. I would have told you."

"I asked Parker about the Cordova Cartel. She clammed up on me. So don't give me that attitude. I know you're hidin' something."

Belle drops the ball between us, then stares from me to AJ and back again before she tries to climb into AJ's lap. He wraps his arms around her, a small smile curving his lips despite having an eighty-pound dog crushing his nuts.

"When have we *not* had an active case against the cartel?" he asks. "Far as I know, there are at least three separate investigations goin' on right now. But I ain't involved in any of them. Neither is Parker."

Well, fuck.

AJ takes a swig from his beer. "You want one?"

"No." That's a bald-faced lie, but I can't shoot the shit with him for the rest of the afternoon—as much as I'd like to. We've talked more this week than in the past eight months combined. "I have to pick Emi up at seven. If she'll let me, I'll bring her out to Grandpappy Blade's cabin. Otherwise, we'll be at her place."

"We?" AJ gives me the side eye. "What the fuck are you doing, Jas? Knockin' boots with the woman who almost blew up the case against the Marquez drug ring? You barely know her!"

I push to my feet. Belle whines, and I reach over and give her sleek head one last stroke. "Since *you* barely know *me* anymore, what I do or don't do with Emi is none of your damn business."

Without waiting for him to say another word, I head for my car. I should have enough time to stop at home, take a shower, and pack a bag for the weekend. If I'm lucky, Emi and I *will* be knockin' boots by the end of the night. But AJ doesn't need to know that.

I'M fresh out of the shower when the six o'clock news comes on. After the initial headlines, the anchor—some guy named Jim Flanagan—stares straight into the camera. "And now, Emmylou Marsh is here with an update on the Empress Hotel and Eugene Fowler controversy. Emmylou?"

The camera pans to Emi sitting next to him. Her bruises are still visible, and she looks exhausted. "Thank you, Jim. Over the past week, we've brought you a story of bribery, corruption, and possible cartel ties with Consolidated Investment Group. Last night, while I was doing my weekly grocery shopping, someone wired a bomb to my car. It went off when I was only steps away."

She stares into the camera, brushing a lock of hair away from her face to reveal the dark purple bruise swelling at her temple. "While I haven't uncovered any other proof linking the cartel to Consolidated Investment Group, the attack on me has their fingerprints all over it."

Goddamnit. She's painting an even bigger target on her back. It only takes me five minutes to get dressed and shove a couple changes of clothes into a duffel bag. I need to get back to Channel 5. Right fucking now.

CHAPTER THIRTEEN

Emi

"The Austin Police Department and the FBI continue to investigate the attack on me and Consolidated Investment Group's connection to the Cordova Cartel. I'll be back on Monday with more on the corruption surrounding the Empress Hotel and Conference Center." I take a slow, steadying breath. This next bit isn't scripted, and Nelson's going to have a coronary over it. Luckily, the studio lights are so bright, I can't see him. "To the individual or individuals who blew up my car last night and almost killed me, I say this. You will not scare me off this story. My duty is to the people of this city. I report the news, and I will not be silenced. Back to you, Jim."

I stare straight into the lens until the red light goes off and the cameraman gives me a nod. In the space of a few seconds, my confidence evaporates into dust. An icy ball of nerves twists in my stomach.

Nelson steps into my line of sight and motions for me to get my ass out of the chair and off set. My hands shake as I struggle to unclip the microphone from my blazer. One of the techs rushes over to help, but I can't take my eyes off of Nelson. His face is bright red, with the veins at his temples throbbing.

"What the hell was that?" he hisses when the broadcast cuts to commercial. "You practically *dared* the cartel to come after you!"

"The networks will pick that up and run with it. When the market share numbers come in, you'll be thanking me," I say with as much strength as I can force into my tone.

"Not if you're dead!" He throws his hands up, then grabs fistfuls of his hair and pulls hard enough his eyes crinkle with pain. "Your story was enough, Emi. And we're twenty-three seconds over time that we have to make up in the C-block."

Of course he'd notice *that*. I don't care. I'd give anything to feel safe again, but this is the opportunity I've been praying for. Cheri almost choked on her gum when I refused to let her touch me with the concealer wand, but my various scrapes and bruises are all part of the story now. From the brief glimpse I caught on the monitors, I look like five miles of bad road. That'll get the networks clamoring for more.

I offer Nelson one of my patented smiles. "Make sure you run the segment as often as possible this weekend. I taped half a dozen different promo spots for you to use, including several that presume they'll come after me again. If you need me to record any updates, give me a call. I'll be hiding out at home until Monday."

His mouth opens and closes several times. "Austin PD isn't offering protective custody?"

I snort. "No. The lead detective told me there was nothing they could do without a credible and consistent threat from *someone they could actually arrest*. I think his exact words were, 'The cartel was sending a message. If they'd truly wanted you dead, you'd be dead.'"

Nelson sputters, but I'm already headed to my office. My little "stunt" on air will likely keep me safer than any rent-a-cop ever could.

Twenty minutes later, after five different people stop me to ask about the attack, my office is finally in sight. "Ms. Marsh?" One of the associate producers rushes down the hall. "There's a guy in the lobby who says he's with you. Jasper Blade? He's demanding that we let him past security."

Shit. He's probably full of piss and vinegar over my report tonight. Sticking my tongue out at the people who tried to kill me won't earn me any points with him. He's too overprotective for his own good.

I rub my left shoulder, one of the bruises throbbing. I could have died last night. I'm still here because Jasper took care of me. Maybe he's exactly the right amount of overprotective.

"Tell him I'll be out in five minutes, Wendy. If he makes a fuss, explain that it takes longer than that to print a guest badge. That should calm him down a bit."

After a quick pit stop in my office to change back into my sweater, then grab my tablet and phone, I push through the security doors. Jasper's pacing, his hands balled into fists at his sides.

Holy shit, the man cleans up well. Dark blue Wranglers, a black vest, and a slate gray button-down shirt. No tie. Leather jacket.

A split second later, he pulls me against him. His muscles relax on an exhale. God, he even smells good. Like a spring waterfall or the prairie after a storm.

"What the hell were you thinkin'?" he asks, but there's no malice in his tone. Only concern.

"I'm a reporter, Jasper. I have an obligation to see the story through to the end. And...if the cartel—or whoever tried to blow me up—knows the FBI is onto them, maybe they'll leave me alone." Drawing back, I trail my fingers over his freshly trimmed beard. "You asked me to be careful. This *is* careful."

"Not careful enough." His kiss is gentle but leaves no question as to how much he wants me. Or...needs me. "You ready to get the fuck out of here?"

"God, yes. Unless there's a fresh break in the story, no one needs me until Monday morning. I can hide out at home all weekend." I leave the last two words unspoken. *With you.*

I don't know if he'll stay. Or if he even wants to. We didn't get that far when we argued over my safety this morning.

Jasper tucks a lock of hair behind my ear. His fingers are warm and rough, but surprisingly gentle. "We'll see about that, sweetheart. I can think of a few other places we could go that might be both private and safe." He punctuates his declaration with a wink. "If you trust me."

I've only known Jasper for a few days, but everything about him *screams* honor. So, I place my hand in his. "I trust you."

Jasper

The little hole-in-the-wall BBQ joint is one of Austin's best kept secrets. With less than fifteen tables, it's still quiet enough on a Saturday night for us to carry on a conversation, and small enough I can keep an eye on the door.

"How long were you a Ranger?" Emi asks as she picks up one of her ribs.

I'd give anything to change the subject, but I promised this woman a proper date, and I intend to deliver. "Almost twelve years. A decade as a State Trooper before that. Me and AJ both."

"Do you and your brother do *everything* together?" Her easy smile is one I could look at for...longer than I should admit after only a week.

A pang of something—regret, sorrow, longing—hits me square in the chest. "We used to. High school football. UT Austin—he studied Criminology. I went for Criminal Justice. I thought I'd become a lawyer."

"A lawyer? Jasper, why didn't you go through with it?" Emi leans forward, a little sparkle in her eyes. If only they weren't still bloodshot from the late night and the concussion.

"I suck at standardized tests. No law school would take a guy who couldn't score above 130 on the LSAT." With a shrug, I reach for my water. God, I'd kill for a beer—or three—right now. But we're out in public, and those sombitches who blew up her car are still in the wind. I have to be at my best if I want to keep her safe.

"So you followed your brother's lead and became a State Trooper."

"Hell, no." With a chuckle, I dig into the plate of brisket. "*He* followed *me*. AJ couldn't decide if he wanted to try for Austin PD or become a trooper so he could end up bein' a Ranger. He went to Spain for two months after we graduated with a couple of his friends, and that's where he met his wife, Grace. She was doing a semester abroad. It was love at first sight. It almost killed him to wait until she graduated college to propose."

Emi lowers her gaze to her plate, and her cheeks turn a shade of pink. "I looked him up at the Boots and Bling event," she says. "Your brother. What happened to him—to Grace..."

"If anyone *knew* what happened to Grace, AJ might be able to find some peace. As it is, he's carryin' a mountain of grief on his shoulders every damn day."

I wish I could tell Emi about the old AJ. The guy who used to love pranks. Who sang karaoke. Who hosted poker parties out at the lake whenever we didn't have to work a long weekend. Hell, I wish I could tell her about the man I talked to this afternoon. The one who could barely muster the will to play with the dog who used to look at Grace like she hung the damn moon.

Struggling for a distraction, I slide the basket of cornbread and maple butter across the table. "The last piece is yours, sweetheart."

Emi bats her eyelashes at me with a wide smile. "Why Jasper Blade, are you trying to *butter me up*?"

"Depends. Is it workin'?"

She plucks the slab of bread from the basket lined with red and white checkered paper. "Come home with me and you can find out."

CHAPTER FOURTEEN

Jasper

THE RIDE from the restaurant to Emi's apartment is the longest of my life. For almost two hours, we ate, talked, and even flirted over BBQ. If the parkin' lot hadn't been so packed, I would have had her up against my truck and kissed the hell out of her once I'd paid the bill. But there'll be plenty of time for that when we're behind locked doors with the blinds drawn.

She ran out of steam halfway to her apartment. Last night's attack, the visit to the police station, her segment, and the food finally catching up to her. "That's your third yawn since we left the restaurant, sweetheart. We're goin' straight to bed when we get to your place."

"Bed, yes," she says as she tries to stifle yet another yawn. "But I have plans for you, Ranger."

"We'll see about that." Emi tries to glare at me, but she's so exhausted, I choke back a laugh. "You'll be asleep before your head hits the pillow."

I LOVE HELPING Emi down from my truck. Her hands rest on my shoulders, while mine mold to her hips. There's nothing sexual about it, but these brief moments are intimate in a way I didn't expect.

"You're a real gentleman," she says softly and brushes a light kiss to my cheek.

"I try, ma'am." Settling my Stetson on my head, I grab my duffel.

"You...packed a bag?" She covers her mouth with her hand, eyes wide.

Fuck me.

"You ain't stayin' alone, Emi. Not with those assholes still out there. I assumed—"

She laughs and runs her fingers through her long, brown locks. "Take a breath, handsome. I was joking."

"Thank fuck. We still haven't finished the conversation we were having in my truck this morning." I rake my eyes up and down Emi's body. Her hip is cocked to one side, her free hand on her waist. My jeans are strangling my dick, and I can't think straight.

An SUV with a squeaky belt rumbles by on the street. Dammit. I didn't hear it coming. Five-feet-six-inches of smart, sassy brunette perfection is all it takes to throw me off my game.

"Inside, Emi. Now."

She fits herself to my side. I'll be lucky if I don't come in my pants before we get in the elevator. Her fingers slide into my back pocket and tighten on my ass. Damn.

The lobby doors unlock after Emi enters her code, but the security desk in front of the elevators is empty. "Where's Benny?"

She glances around the atrium. "He usually takes a break around nine. He's probably getting something to eat. Or talking to his daughter. She's a lawyer out in California. I'm sure he'll be back in a few minutes."

I don't give a fuck if Benny is smoking a joint behind the dumpster or fucking his girlfriend in the supply closet. Something in the air doesn't feel right, but I can't put my finger on it.

Emi digs her hand deeper into my pocket. Those warm brown eyes meet mine for a brief moment before she punches in her code for the elevator and the doors whisper open. "Come upstairs, Jasper."

I push her against the wall of the car. With my hands wrapped around her waist, I claim her mouth. A single flick of my tongue against her lips and she opens for me.

Last night, she tried to keep as much space between us as possible. Tonight, she can't get close enough and wraps one leg around my thigh.

The doors open with a *ding*. We move as one into the hall. Emi fumbles around in her bag, and her keys escape, crashing to the floor.

I keep a hand tight around her hip as I ease myself down to one knee, scoop up the ring, and pass it to her. "We gotta get inside. Right fucking now."

"Then let me open the door, handsome." She winks, then slides the key into the lock.

At the last second, my brain wrestles control away from my dick. Covering her hand with mine, I shake my head. "Get behind me. Gotta clear the place first." Confusion clouds her gaze, and I add, "I need to make sure no one's been here since this morning."

"You think...?" The arousal in her eyes fades in an instant. "Benny wouldn't have let anyone on the elevator. And if my security system had gone off, he'd have called me."

"Unless it happened in the past ten minutes." I tug the leg of my jeans up a couple of inches and slide the small Glock from my ankle holster. "Breathe, sweetheart. I'm sure it's safe. But I'd be a damn fool not to check."

"Jasper, the door was locked. You're overreacting. Let's just go inside."

She's gone from flirty to exasperated in seconds. Before I can stop her, she pushes the door open. "Emi, wait—"

Two steps into her apartment, everything goes sideways and ass backwards.

A black-gloved hand grabs Emi's wrist and jerks her forward. I throw my entire body against the door, hoping to unbalance whomever's lying in wait on the other side.

The wood hits something solid. I spin around, landing a right hook to a skinny fucker's jaw. His eyes roll back in his head, and he collapses as another man comes into view. His voice sends ice sinking like a glacier in my gut.

"Move, and she dies."

Emi

The sickening mix of sweat and cologne burns my nose. My head spins. Something hard slams against my temple, and I see stars. Off balance, I stumble—no, I'm pulled—backwards. One of my shoes is gone. Where...?

Something...an arm?...bands around my neck. It's hard to swallow. Hard to breathe.

"Emi!" Jasper shouts. The apartment door bangs shut.

"Drop the gun," a man grits out, his voice only inches from my ear.

Panic swims in Jasper's dark blue eyes for a beat. But then he swallows hard, holds his hands away from his sides, and slowly lowers the small pistol to the floor.

"Now kick it away."

This isn't happening. It's not real. It can't be real.

The gun skids across the floor. I watch it spin, my gaze pinned to the black metal. My throw pillows are in shreds. Half my kitchen cabinets are open. The whole place looks like a tornado tore through it.

"Not the sharpest tools in the shed, are you?" Jasper asks, his voice a hell of a lot calmer than it should be.

I want to scream, but I can't. All I can do is try to loosen the arm cutting off my air. The guy holding me slams the barrel of the gun against the swollen knot on my forehead. The world goes soft, and I fight to keep my knees from buckling.

"Shut the fuck up. Do exactly what we say, and maybe you'll walk out of here alive."

Jasper laughs. His entire body trembles with the sound. I'm surprised tears aren't streaming from his eyes.

We're going to die! What the hell is so funny?

No one's coming to our rescue. Jasper gave up his gun. The man behind him is still unconscious, but how much longer will *that* last? I'm so dizzy, I'd be on the floor if it weren't for the arm around my neck.

"You think I'm joking?" the man asks. He takes a step back, dragging me with him. We're almost to the living room now.

I claw at him, but he's wearing a jacket *and* gloves. My feeble efforts do nothing but piss him off. He tightens his grip. I start to wheeze.

"Listen, shit for brains," Jasper says. "You tried to blow up Emi's car. The FBI and Austin PD are on to you. There's no way in hell you'll let either of us walk out of here alive. I know it. You know it. But that gives *me* the advantage. Because I've got nothin' left to lose." Jasper lowers his hands to his sides and takes one step toward me.

The asshole drags me halfway to the living room window. What happens when there's nowhere left to go?

"Don't come any closer," he says. Some of the bravado has faded from his voice. "You know who we work for, Mr. Blade. We can do whatever the fuck we want. But we don't like killing women. Not unless we have to. Give us the recording and we'll—"

His arm is getting tighter by the second. Panic takes over. "P-please," I beg. "I don't have—"

"Where is it?" he roars at me.

"Wh-where's what?" Dark spots float at the edges of my vision. Nothing feels real anymore. I'm here, but not. My heartbeat races, pounding in my ears.

Halfway across the room, Jasper calls my name. "Emi. Look at me, sweetheart. Right now." He flicks his gaze down to the floor and back up again. "Everything's gonna be okay. Trust me."

It's not. It's *so* not. Why is he so confident? Oh, God. He looks down at the floor again. Is he trying to tell me something?

Jasper takes another step toward us. His body angles slightly. "If she passes out, you sure as shit won't get whatever it is you came here for."

I'm so dizzy—almost hyperventilating. I *could* pass out.

With a weak moan, I let my head loll onto my chest. My knees give way. The hold around my neck loosens, and the ground rushes up to meet me.

Jasper moves so fast, he's only a dark blur. Something clatters to the floor, followed by a heavy *thud*.

Blood. I smell blood. It's so close. My back hits the window. The gunman rolls from side to side, gurgling. Choking. Jasper kicks the pistol across the room.

Blood seeps through the man's fingers, dripping onto the floor. Something silver glints in the light. A knife. *It's sticking out of his throat.*

His mouth opens and closes. Every second, his movements are weaker. Until they stop entirely and his hands fall away.

"He's...dead!" I try to get up, but the room spins. My stomach roils. "Jasper...what did you do?"

"It was either him or us, and I wasn't gonna let him hurt you." Jasper's in front of me now. Gently, he frames my face with his big, warm hands, and then his lips are on mine. Just a hint of pressure. So light that once he pulls back, I wonder if I imagined the kiss entirely. "Say somethin', sweetheart."

Before I can, there's a moan from across the room.

Jasper jerks his head around, and I swear he actually *growls*. Yet once he returns his focus to me, he's so tender. Like he thinks I'm about to shatter. I probably am.

"Do you have any duct tape?" he asks.

"Huh? Wh-what?" I can't take my eyes off the other man. The one who's still alive.

"Duct tape, Emi. You have some?"

His tone snaps me out of the panic threatening to pull me under. "Kitchen. The drawer to the left of the sink."

"If I help you up, can you get it for me? I ain't so sure that fucker's gonna stay down." He wraps an arm around my waist, lifts me to my feet, and holds me until my vision clears.

"I'm okay," I whisper.

In truth, "okay" might as well be on Jupiter. But Jasper saved our lives, and I have to help him.

Kicking off my other shoe, I stumble into the kitchen. Jasper flips the semi-conscious man onto his stomach and pins his hands to the small of his back. Nothing is where it should be. I find the duct tape on the floor in front of the sink. Once I have it in my hands, I freeze. My gaze locks on the man by the window. The blood. The knife still stuck in his throat.

"We have to call the police..." I manage.

"No." Jasper holds out his hand. "Bring me the duct tape. Tear off a strip at least four feet long. I can do the rest."

Despite my confusion, I do as he says. The man under him struggles weakly. My heart starts to race. Jasper wraps the tape around the guy's wrists, then takes the roll from me and hogties him.

"Go pack whatever you need for a couple of nights. Essentials only. We have to get the fuck out of here. Five minutes and we're gone. You understand?"

"What about...?" Gesturing to the dead man, I shudder. His face is almost peaceful.

"I'm callin' for reinforcements."

CHAPTER FIFTEEN

Jasper

I CAN HEAR Emi moving around in the bedroom over the muffled curses from the duct-taped idjit on the floor.

"You're doin' a hell of a lot better than your partner over there," I say, keeping my voice low. "You want to keep it that way? Shut up."

Punctuating my threat by slamming his head against the table leg next to him, I regret the pleasure the act of violence gives me. I should be a better man. But the fucker could have killed us both. He *would* have if I'd been a second slower. So the remorse fades by the time I've fished out my phone and punched in AJ's number.

"What the fuck do you want?" AJ grits out. "I'm...busy."

"Not anymore you ain't. Send a couple of your guys to 301 Liberty Road. Apartment 608. Get the coroner too."

"Jasper, are you okay?" The frustration, hurt, and anger fall away in an instant, and he's family again. Damn if that doesn't make me feel even worse about what I'm getting him into.

"For now. The fuckwits who blew up Emi's car last night just came after her again. That address I gave you is her apartment. And before you start hollarin' at me, the knife sticking out of the dead guy's neck is mine. My prints are all over it. It was self-defense."

"You were defending *yourself*? Or Emi?" After a beat, he snorts. "Don't answer that. Not without a lawyer. I'm going to catch so much shit for this. You damn well better be there when Billings and McGrath show up. Let 'em arrest you. I'll call in a couple of favors and get Carson Poole to represent you. He'll have you out within an hour or two."

"Goddammit, AJ. I'm not stayin' here and you will *not* call Poole. I'm takin' Emi somewhere safe. Get a car with clean plates and meet me at the Silver Tower Hotel on Grand in an hour. They have an underground parking garage with very few blind spots. Only one way in and out. Easy to keep watch. You see any sign of a tail, you stay the fuck away and call me immediately."

My brother swears under his breath. "If whatever you're tangled up in ruins my career, Jas, I swear to fuck I will beat your ass into next week."

The phone beeps twice, and I stare at the screen. He hung up on me. Fucking hell.

"Jasper?" I turn to Emi. She changed into a pair of yoga pants, a sweatshirt, and running shoes. A tear glistens on her cheek, and she pulls a small, rolling suitcase behind her. "What does 'a car with clean plates' mean?"

With a quick glance at the unconscious man on the floor, I shake my head. "Not here, sweetheart. I'll explain on the way. Let's go."

In the hall, I stop her before she can slide her key into the lock. "Rangers are on the way. You want them bustin' the door down? Because that's what they'll do if they can't get in. Leave it open, and they'll probably lock up when they leave."

"I can't... What about...*him*?" she hisses. "He could get away."

"Not with how well I tied him up." I level a gaze at her. "*This part*, I know, Emi. I may not be 'on the job' anymore, but my skills didn't disappear because I got blown up. He's not going anywhere."

She nods. Seconds later, AJ texts me.

AJ: Billings and McGrath are seven minutes out.

Shit. "Gotta go. Right now. I'll...ask AJ to lock up." I grab her suitcase and head for the elevator.

"This is a nightmare." Her earlier anger has been tempered by exhaustion. Pain pinches her brows. "Where are you taking me?"

The words are so quiet, I barely hear them, but I can't stand the defeat marring her tone.

"We're gonna go to a hotel to meet my brother. Then I'm takin' you to our family cabin at Lake Livingston."

Back in the lobby, Benny's desk is still empty. It's been way too long for him to still be on a smoke break. "Those two were probably acting alone. But stay behind me. Hand on my hip. Or hold onto my belt loop. Okay?"

"No. I can't go to your cabin, Jasper. And I won't hide from the police. I'm a reporter. If I break the law—if I run—how is the public ever supposed to trust me again?" She jams her hands on her hips. "Eugene Fowler—and his cartel connections—don't get to scare me off my own damn story."

I cup her cheek. "Emi, they would have killed you tonight. I'm not asking you to walk away from the story. But you can't report on *anything* if you're dead. Trust me. Please."

She flinches, but after a beat, a sigh heaves her shoulders. "Okay. But we can't just go to a hotel?"

"Hotels use credit cards. The cartel would be onto us within an hour. The cabin is the safest place I know. And it's far enough from Austin to buy us a couple of days for AJ to find out who sent them after you in the first place. Stay close. We're going to my truck. Right now."

Thank fuck there was an open guest spot close to the door. Emi climbs into the passenger seat while I throw her suitcase and my duffel into the lockbox.

"I know who sent them," she says softly when I'm behind the wheel. "Eugene Fowler and Consolidated Investment Group. The death threats started after my interview with him."

Fuck. It takes all I have to force a deep breath. "The FBI didn't offer you *any* protection?"

"You and my news director. Eternal optimists," she mutters. "No. They can't help me. Or won't. Honestly, I think they just want my sources. If I gave those up, I'd have 24/7 guards by now."

The truck rumbles to life, and I pull out onto the main road. My gaze pings from one mirror to the next, clocking the make, model, and color of every car on the road. Retired almost a year, and I slip back into old habits like I never left the Rangers.

"You really think the Feds are withholding protection for a source?" I ask. In the next second, I shake my head. "Of course they are. Fucking idiots. You got real intel on Fowler and CIG in what? A month? Two?"

"Five weeks. More or less."

Shit. She's a goddamn badass. Brilliant. Driven. And *mine*.

"Do you know how many times the Rangers tried to take Fowler and his companies down? AJ's gonna shit himself." I glance over at her, worried at the way she's leaning against the side window, her eyelids drooping.

"Why?" she asks.

"Because the Cordova Cartel owned that warehouse on Grand. They killed Schaffer and Urbanski. I wasn't even supposed to be there. It was AJ's case. Would have been if...well, if he'd had his head on straight. He'd do anything to take those fuckers down."

Emi

When did my life turn in to a TV movie-of-the-week? Yes, I wanted the story to go national. Yes, I wanted to bring down a corrupt developer I *know* has been hurting and exploiting people for years.

And yes...I *had* secretly wondered how bad it would be if someone actually *did* try to kill me. That probably wasn't smart.

I'm so tired. I'd managed to forget about most of my bruises while Jasper and I flirted over dinner. Now, my entire body aches. Every time I move my head, I remember the arm around my neck cutting off my air. The gun jamming against my temple.

I curl deeper into the seat of Jasper's truck with a shiver. He glances over at me, then cranks the heat in the cab. "You doing okay, sweetheart?"

"Where are we going?" I tug at the sleeves of my sweatshirt, needing something to do with my hands. I think Jasper's driving in circles. Turning so often, I'm almost dizzy. "And what are 'clean plates'?"

He checks the rearview mirror, changes lanes, and checks again. "AJ spends his weekends out by Lake Travis. We're just lolly-gaggin' for a bit until he can get back into town. He's got resources I don't. Including access to a car that ain't registered to me, you, or anyone these fuckers can trace back to us."

"Us?" My voice cracks, and my hands are so cold, I can't feel my fingers.

Jasper merges onto the freeway and floors it, his face a grim mask of determination and purpose. "The guy I killed knew my name, Emi. These assholes are connected, and they ain't gonna stop until *someone* makes them."

———

HALF AN HOUR LATER, Jasper pulls the truck into an underground parking garage, finds a spot near the elevator, and kills the engine.

There can't be more than ten other vehicles in the entire lot, and by the way his gaze moves from car to car, I think he memorizes all of them before he comes around to the passenger side to open my door.

"We're gonna go book a room, but then we're coming right back here," he says and motions for me to slide to the edge of the seat so he can help me down.

"I look like shit. I should..." I gesture to my face and reach for the visor.

He cups my cheek, gently skimming his thumb just under my eye. "This is gonna sound as rude as hell, but the bruises will help the desk clerk remember you. We want anyone who comes lookin' to be absolutely positive you're *here* and not where we're going."

"Well, that's not terrifying at all."

"Fuck." Jasper stiffens and balls his hands into fists. "AJ was always better at being...reassuring."

"I'd rather you be honest than tell me what you think I need to hear." I try for a smile, but it's painfully obvious he doesn't believe me. As we head for the elevator, he keeps me tucked against his side, protected. Like I'm precious. Cared for.

How did we get here so fast? It's been seven days—if you don't count the fifteen minutes we spent together all those months ago. He shouldn't be the most important person in my world. Yet, that's where we are.

Oh, God. This is absolutely a *Lifetime Movie of the Week* scenario. If I hadn't almost died twice in the past forty-eight hours, I'd laugh. Instead, all I want to do is hide away somewhere with Jasper until he tells me it's safe. Because he's the only person I know I can trust.

TEN MINUTES LATER, we're back in his truck, a plastic room key on the dashboard. The clerk didn't just recognize me. He asked for my autograph. If he's not texting all his friends right now, it'll be a miracle.

Jasper peers at his phone, shakes his head, and mutters, "Dammit, AJ. The gas pedal is on the right. Try usin' it once in a while."

It's cold with the engine off, and I pull my sleeves down over my hands. I haven't been warm since we left my apartment. I'm not sure I'll ever be warm again the way things are going. If the console weren't in the way, I'd snuggle up to Jasper's side. Or ask him to put his arms around me.

A pair of headlights flash in the rear view mirror. "Slouch down, Emi," Jasper says, an edge to his tone. "Just in case."

"Are you seriously telling me to get on the floor?" If my face—

or my entire body—didn't hurt like hell right now, I'd arch my brows and glare at him. But I'm too tired. Instead, I ease myself down until I'm crouching on the floorboards.

After a beat, he leans over and presses a kiss to the top of my head. "It's AJ. You can get up now. I'll be right around to help you out."

Jasper's twin parks a small, blue SUV two spaces away. God, they look so much alike. Though AJ's hair is darker. He doesn't have a beard. Just rough stubble. And when he gets closer, I can see a lifetime of pain in the blue depths of his eyes.

"Emi, this is my brother, Aaron." Jasper reaches out to clasp the man on the shoulder briefly.

"No one calls me that anymore. It's AJ," he says before passing Jasper a set of keys. "The SUV belongs to Parker's roommate, so try not to destroy it."

"Who's Parker?" I ask.

"One of the Rangers I work with. She's good people. Despite how often she rats me out to my *little* brother." AJ glares at Jasper. "That stops. Now. You hear?"

"Give me your driver's license," Jasper says, completely ignoring his brother's question. Digging into the back pocket of his jeans, he comes up with his own license and the credit card he used to pay for our room.

I catch a quick glimpse of AJ's ID as the two men exchange glances. *Aaron Jasper Stone.* There's a story here I'm going to investigate. After I sleep. Because right now, my brain feels like mush. It's getting harder and harder to focus on the conversation happening right in front of me. The one where Jasper's telling AJ something about going "off the grid" for a while.

I don't know how I get into the borrowed SUV. Or when we leave the garage. Only that Jasper's leather jacket is draped over me, and I'm finally warm. The lull of the engine drags me under, and I don't fight my need to sleep. Jasper will protect me.

CHAPTER SIXTEEN

Jasper

IT'S A THREE-HOUR DRIVE, and Emi doesn't stir once. Not even when I stop the car to unlock the security gate.

The cabins at Lake Livingston aren't what most folks expect. No one comes up here to "get away from it all" anymore. Most places have high-speed internet and satellite television. There's a gourmet grocery store five miles back, and a Michelin-starred restaurant twenty minutes away.

Fifty years ago, Grandpappy Blade built this place himself. Back then, the cabin had two rooms and an outhouse. Now? More than once I've thought about moving up here permanently. It's a hell of a lot nicer than my apartment.

I let Emi sleep until I've unlocked the front door and disarmed the security system.

A soft moan escapes her lips as I slide an arm under her thighs. "Shh, sweetheart. We're here. Don't worry."

"What...time is it?" she slurs.

"A little after 2:00 a.m. I'll have you in bed in a hot minute." I nudge the SUV's door closed with my elbow and carry Emi inside.

She settles her head against my shoulder with a little sigh. "We're safe here?"

"As safe as we can be. We're three hours from Austin and no one knows about this place but me and AJ. Well, and our mama, but she's on a Caribbean cruise for the next week." Emi shivers as I set her down on the bed. "Get under the covers. I'll have the heat goin' in a minute or two."

"And...then you'll come back. Right?" She peers up at me, her eyes bloodshot, the bags underneath them twice the size they were when we left Austin.

Fuck me. Less than four hours ago, we were on a date. I thought we'd be naked in her bed right now. But she's too vulnerable. Too scared. In too much pain for me to do anything but sleep on the couch tonight.

"I'll come check on you. But after that, I'll be in the living room." I lean down and press a kiss to her forehead. "You need to rest."

"I'll sleep—if you're with me." She grabs my hands, twining our fingers. "I don't want to be alone, Jasper. And we had this same fight yesterday. Turn on the heat, then come to bed."

My dick strains against my zipper. This woman is perfect. Strong. Confident. Yet still vulnerable. And sexy as fuck wrapped in my leather jacket. I'd like to see her in that—and nothing else.

"I need to lock up and get our bags. There's a security fence all around the property, along with motion lights, cameras, and alarms. No one's gettin' in here without us knowin' about it."

The worry pinching her features fades slightly, and she sinks against the pillows. "Okay. If you're sure we're safe..."

"I am. And I'll be back in two shakes." I slide my fingers into her hair, tip her head back, and claim her lips. Her cool hand cups my neck, holding me close long enough to sweep her tongue against mine.

"I'll be counting."

Walking away from her is actively painful. By the time I bring in our bags, turn on the heat, and arm the security system, my own exhaustion has caught up with me. Along with the agony setting fire to my hip. Hell, my whole damn leg feels like I've been hit by a truck.

Emi's shoes peek out from under the bed, and in the bathroom, one of the new toothbrushes from the cabinet is unwrapped.

Good. She made herself at home. I tear the plastic off a second brush and try to scrub the disgusting gas station coffee off my tongue. I hated leaving her for even a minute, but it was either that or drive us into a ditch outside of College Station.

Just one more thing to do. The safe in the closet holds enough firepower to defend against a small army. I find a SIG P320, snap the loaded magazine into place, and set it on the nightstand. The revolver from my ankle holster slides between the mattress and the headboard.

This cabin might have every modern convenience, but I won't take any chances with Emi's life. Not after tonight. Because in only a week, she's gone from a complete stranger to someone I'm falling for.

This shouldn't happen. Love at first sight—or almost first sight—is romance novel-type shit. Sure, AJ and Grace found it. But they lived a charmed life until Grace disappeared.

I never believed in true love. But now? I might need to change my tune. If the past couple of years have taught me and AJ anything, it's that life is too fucking short to wait around when you know what you want.

Emi doesn't stir when I shed my jeans and button-down shirt. Sleeping next to her in just my boxer briefs again? This could end...badly. Because I'm going to pull her against me and hold her all night long.

AJ and I each keep a couple of changes of clothes in the closet and dresser. I find a pair of checkered flannel pajama pants and tug them on. These will have to do. For now.

Emi sighs and snuggles up to me as soon as I lie down. She's wearing a tank top and panties—but nothing else—and her soft curves feel so right against me. When we're safe again, I'm askin'

Emmylou Marsh out on a second date. I hope to all that's holy in this world, she says yes.

A LITTLE AFTER NINE, Emi shuffles out into the cabin's main room, yawning the whole way. She's back in yoga pants and a sweatshirt. Damn. I'm almost disappointed.

"There's coffee?" she asks.

"Instant. But it'll do." I set my mug down and start the electric kettle. Emi joins me, leaning her hip against the counter to stare out at the glassy water.

"It's so quiet here. I bet it's hopping over the summer."

I give her coffee a stir, then press the cup into her hands. "My grandfather got lucky when he bought this place. The lot is twice as big as most of the others. This late in the season, the vacation rentals drop off, and the only folks left are the retirees who live up here full time."

Emi's eyelids flutter at the first sip of coffee. "I don't think I've slept that hard in ages."

Sliding my arm around her back, I pull her close and press a kiss to her forehead. "You needed it. Still do, I reckon."

She sighs against me. "I'm fine, Jasper. Just sore. And hungry. Is there anything to eat?"

Reluctantly, I release her and move to the cabinet next to the stove. "Oatmeal. We keep the freezer stocked, but I didn't think to take out any bacon last night."

After I refill the kettle, I grab the tin of oatmeal and a couple of bowls. "Sit down, sweetheart. AJ got us burner phones, so you can call your news director—or anyone else you need—after you eat."

She chews on her lip for a moment, then shuffles over to the table and pulls out one of the chairs. "I'm worried about Kyle. My cameraman," she clarifies. "He wasn't mentioned in any of the death threats, but he was worried enough to transfer to Midday. I'm sure Nelson has updated his security detail, but I should still check on him."

"Tell me about the death threats. And why you weren't worried about them before the other night." It doesn't matter how long I've been off the job. I fall back into the role easily. I miss it. Though I'd give anything not to need these skills right now.

Emi takes another sip of coffee, then sighs. "I used to work for the biggest news station in Los Angeles, Jasper. Death threats were a rite of passage. Once you got your first, you were a legit reporter. I was covering national news back then. Government corruption, politics, serial killers. Austin local news is small potatoes."

"What did the threats say? Do you remember?" Despite how little sleep I got last night, I'm wide awake now. And then it hits me. I went to bed stone cold sober for the second night in a row. My leg aches like a sombitch, but it's manageable.

I've been a borderline alcoholic for months now. I never blacked out. Never *craved* a beer. But I used it to dull the pain. Every damn day. Until Emi needed me.

"Jasper? Are you even listening?" Emi asks, curling her fingers around my wrist. The contact sends a spark of electricity racing up my arm.

"Shit. Sorry, sweetheart. Didn't realize I was so hungry. Go on." I mix up two bowls of oatmeal, then carry them back to the table. She follows, but eyes me suspiciously. "Promise," I say after I wash my first bite of nearly flavorless paste down with another swig of coffee. "That's all it was."

From her expression, she's not convinced, but she runs a hand through her hair and turns her gaze to the window. "The first one was almost comical. 'Leave Eugene Fowler alone.'" She tries for a chuckle, but her shoulders are hiked up close to her ears. "Like we were bullying him in the school yard or something. We got dozens like that the first day, but only one of them from an anonymous email account with no name attached to it."

She scrapes up a bit of her own oatmeal, stares at it for a beat, then sets the spoon down. "The network's social media accounts were being hammered nonstop."

"The story ran for three nights?" I ask.

With a nod, Emi stirs her oatmeal. She still hasn't taken a bite.

"Everything went sideways when the second segment aired. I found evidence of Fowler's corruption back in Chicago. One of the construction workers who worked on the Filagree Tower Hotel sent me a picture of Fowler meeting with a member of the Ricci crime family. The guy claimed more than half of the crew on that project was non-union, and I was able to confirm that the Texas Laborers union had only sent twenty of their members to the Empress job, but there are at least fifty people on the payroll. The threats started getting a lot more...explicit after that. Calling me a whore, saying they were going to come down to the station and show me how a woman was *supposed* to act..."

Anger tightens a vise grip around my heart. I clench my fists and shove them under the table before I say—or do—something I'll regret. Like tell Emi there's no way she's ever goin' on the air again. I know that's not the right answer. But it's the only one I've got at the moment.

I'd like to drag those fuckers out behind the barn and teach them some manners. Bein' able to say your piece from behind a computer or a phone makes people a hundred times meaner and a thousand times braver.

"There were plenty of supportive messages too, don't get me wrong." After a quick glance at me, she returns her focus to the bowl and finally takes her first bite. "The FBI was *very* interested in what I had on Fowler, and tried to pressure me to give up all my sources. I shared what I could—anyone I'd named on air, a few of the documents that were public record, that sort of thing. The last I heard from Agent Van, they were going to bring Fowler in for questioning. But...that was the day my car blew up. I tried to call him yesterday and it went to voicemail."

She grimaces at her second spoonful of oatmeal, then carries the bowl to the sink. I follow, wrap my arm around her waist, and press a kiss to the top of her head. God, when she leans against me, it's like I'm home. Like I'm right where I'm meant to be. "AJ might be able to find out who sent the death threats. Can you show them to me?"

"I'll get my tablet." She heads for the bedroom, and a moment later, there's a muffled curse.

Fuck. I probably should have warned her that I disabled the cell and wifi connections on her devices.

"Jasper? Did you mess with this?" With the tablet held aloft, she stares me down.

"I did, and I'd do it again. No one knows we're up here, Emi. And I aim to keep it that way. It ain't as easy as TV and movies make it sound to track your phone, but the cartel has more money than God himself. They could get it done without breakin' a sweat."

I don't remember when I wrapped my hands around Emi's hips, but now that we're here—no space at all between us—I'm hyper aware of every breath. Of her scent. Jasmine and vanilla. Of the way she's staring up at me. Half spitfire ready to take on the world, half wounded bird in need of protecting.

"Thank you."

I'm ready to continue my tirade, but her words stop me short. "You're not angry?"

"No." Emi rests her cheek against my chest. "I was. For a hot minute. And then I realized why you did it." A sigh escapes her lips. "I've interviewed serial killers and members of MS-13. I've run from a group of gang members who were so angry we caught them on camera, they shot at us."

"Fuckin' A, Emi. Why do you do this job?"

This is the question that riles her up.

"Because I'm good at it." She's madder than a newly branded bull, and shoves at my chest until I release her. "Because someone has to report the news. There's a reason we're called the *Fourth Estate*. We keep those who want unchecked power from taking it. When we do our jobs, anyway. Journalism *means* something, Jasper. Don't ask me to quit. Because I won't. Not for anyone or anything."

"Emi—"

"No. Don't take that tone with me. You spent more than twenty years in law enforcement, and it almost killed you. Double standard much?"

She's right. But I can't see past my worry to admit it. I should walk away, but my heart already has its bags packed for the Emi Marsh Express, and I can't stop myself. Arms crossed over my chest, I dig in, ready to die on this hill if I have to.

"I don't know what it's like where you come from, Emmylou, but here in Texas, men don't stand back and watch our women put themselves in danger without sayin' a goddamn word."

"Where I come from?" Emi's voice takes on a thick, Texas twang. "Well, bless your little chauvinistic heart, Jasper Blade. I grew up spittin' distance from this here lake. So I know what Texas men are like. And for your information, some of them are downright enlightened these days. Until just now, I thought you were one of them."

I should apologize. But I'm so shocked by the change in her voice, the unmistakable drawl, and that's all I can focus on. "What the hell just happened? A minute ago, you were all citified and now...?"

"You try makin' it to the national news networks with a southern accent. We—women, especially—are supposed to be the girl next door. *Everyone's* girl next door. In my business, standing out for anything other than your looks is frowned upon. I hired a voice coach after I graduated college. It worked, too. Got me all the way to an offer with the United Broadcasting Network in New York City." Her words falter. She stares up at the ceiling and swallows hard. "And then my grandmother got sick. My sister lives in the UK, so I turned down the offer from UBN and moved back here. Grams died almost a year ago. But eighteen months is practically an eternity in network news, so now, I'm stuck here. I can't even get an interview back in L.A., let alone New York."

"Why not?" Taking a risk, I offer her my hand. After a long moment, she lets me lead her to the couch, but though she sits next to me, she holds herself stiffly, like she's worried if she lets go, even for a minute, she'll shatter.

"Too long working this small, local market." She shakes her

head when I open my mouth to protest. "Austin *is* small compared to Los Angeles. At least that's the perception. Any big, national network wants pretty young things who'll take pennies compared to the male reporters. I'm stuck here. Unless I cover a story so sensational, New York is forced to pay attention. Fowler? *That's* one that could get me there. And I ain't givin' it up because some asshole crook is all hat and no cattle."

Easing her closer, I slide my fingers into her hair and gently tip her head back. "Sweetheart, I should never have asked you to stop doing your job. I fucked this all up because I want to keep you safe. Because you're my whole world right now, and I think we have a chance for something...long term. If you're willing..."

Emi's bow lips purse as she holds my gaze. "Are you sure you're not saying that because we almost died two nights in a row?"

"Did you just try to compare us to Keanu Reeves and Sandra Bullock in *Speed*?" I shift my weight so I can pull her into my lap, and she doesn't resist. "Because that movie had a happy ending."

"I'm *trying* to be realistic." Her eyes flutter, and before I can lean down to kiss her, she cups the back of my neck and brings her lips to mine.

Never in my life has such a tame kiss set my body on fire so fast. I want more. So much more. Hell, I want everything with this woman.

Maybe even...a lifetime.

CHAPTER SEVENTEEN

Emi

Kissing Jasper was a mistake. A glorious, fireworks-inducing, hormone-revving mistake. Because now that I'm in the shower—alone—all I want is for him to join me.

Though when I reach up to rinse the shampoo from my hair, my bruises protest the movement. Maybe naked fun can wait until tonight. Assuming Jasper has some ibuprofen around here somewhere.

I escaped to the bathroom when he started reading all the emails and social media comments Channel 5 received after my story started running. Each one kicked his anger up a notch—or five. He wasn't mad at *me*, but it's a good thing Eugene Fowler isn't anywhere around here. I'm afraid Jasper would beat the everlovin' shit out of the corrupt wannabe-Texan.

Once I'm dressed in a pair of black leggings and a soft green sweater, I pull my hair up into a messy bun and pad back out to the main room. Maybe Jasper's heard from his brother by now.

But the cabin is empty. Quiet. My tablet sits on the table next to a folded piece of paper.

Catching a couple of fish for lunch. You'll be able to see me out the kitchen window. - Jas

The counter is cool against my palms as I steady myself on my toes to peer outside. My protector stands on a wooden dock with his back to me. His heavy winter coat can't hide an ass perfectly framed by tight Wranglers.

He reels in the line with a fat, wriggling fish on the other end, and within five seconds, dumps it into a bucket at his side.

His Stetson shadows his eyes when he turns back to the cabin, but the look of peace on his face is...beautiful. There's no other word for it. *He's* beautiful. Handsome and strong and rugged...and —for today, at least—mine.

"I think we have a chance for somethin'...long term."

Long term. How can he possibly be thinking long term when we've known each other for a week?

The same way you can.

Last night, when he climbed into bed with me, all I wanted was to be close to him. Some of that was probably my desperate need to keep my memories at bay. The gun pressed to my temple. The arm around my neck. My life flashing before my eyes. Turns out that actually *is* a thing.

But that wasn't the only reason I wanted his arms around me. With Jasper, I feel like I'm the only woman in this world—in *his* world. He wouldn't give a shit if I stopped covering the gray in my hair—or even lost my entire career tomorrow. It wouldn't change a thing between us.

"Ready for a halfway decent meal?" he asks as he locks the door behind him. "Not much bitin' this time of year, but the catfish are always hungry."

"You know how to cook...that?" Gesturing to the bucket, I take a step back. I may be from Texas, but I prefer not to see my food in its *original* form. Or while it's still wriggling.

He chuckles. "This cabin's been in my family for fifty years. AJ and I spent every summer weekend up here. I caught my first bass when I was..." he rubs his chin, and his fingers rasp over his thick beard, "six years old. By the time I was nine, Grandpappy made sure I knew how to clean, prep, and cook the fish too."

"You haven't mentioned your dad once," I say as Jasper transfers the fish to a utility sink in a small room off the kitchen. "Did he spend weekends up here too?"

Jasper's shoulders go rock hard, and he shakes his head. "Nope. He wasn't around much when we were growin' up. He worked as a long-haul trucker until he got into a wreck on I-90 outside of Rapid City. Fucked up his back so he couldn't drive anymore. Our mama—she was a teacher—had to take a second job at night down at the liquor store to pay the bills."

"Is he still...around?"

With a snort, Jasper slices the head off the first fish. "The year we graduated high school, he went to jail for possession with intent to sell. The asshole left Mama with a mountain of debt. AJ was fit to be tied. Marched down to the courthouse the day after the trial ended to change his last name. Stone is Mama's maiden name."

Well, that explains part of the mystery.

"Why didn't you change yours too?" I ask.

Jasper slides the knife down the fish's belly. I pin my gaze to his face so I don't have to look at what *used* to be inside our impending lunch. "I should have. But I was young and stupid. I thought if I were a good enough trooper, I could somehow make up for all the pain our pops caused."

"Jasper, that wasn't your responsibility."

My words hit him like a physical blow, and his shoulders jerk.

"Maybe not. But..." Shrugging, he moves on to the second fish. "AJ called while I was out there. No one showed up at the hotel last night lookin' for us. But Austin PD took over the case from the Ranger Division, and they have me listed as a person of interest for the dead guy at your apartment. The other one ain't talkin'. Probably too scared the cartel will silence him permanently."

"Shit. What you did...it was self-defense. I need to call Detective Mitchell." I turn back to the kitchen in search of one of the burner phones AJ gave us.

"Emi, no." Jasper's protest stops me before I can dial. "Until we know for sure who sent those assholes after you, I don't trust *anyone* but AJ. He called in a few favors, and got a look at the evidence against Consolidated Investment Group and Eugene Fowler. It's solid. He can't figure out what the FBI's waitin' for. They should have arrested him by now."

I lean against the counter, the stress crawling up the back of my neck until my head starts to throb.

"So...we're not going back to Austin tonight. Or any time soon."

I'm equal parts disappointed and excited. Spending time with Jasper—here, where no one can get to us and we can just be ourselves—is wonderful. But before long, I'll have to return to Channel 5, and I'd rather not do that with a target on my back.

"It's not safe, sweetheart," Jasper says softly. "If I bring you to my place, chances are, I'll be arrested. Your apartment is still a crime scene. Austin PD found Benny tied up in a supply closet with a broken arm and a concussion. He's gonna be okay, but these assholes clearly don't mind hurting anyone who gets in their way. And we still don't know what they wanted from you last night."

I sink down into one of the kitchen chairs and drop my head into my hands. "Then after lunch, I need to call Nelson."

<hr>

THE FISH WAS EXCELLENT—AND Jasper surprised me by pulling a bunch of kale out of the fridge—*my* bunch of kale he'd apparently liberated from my apartment the night before.

Despite the company—and the food—by the time we finish the dishes, I'm about to come out of my skin. "Call him," Jasper says, sliding one of the phones across the counter to me. "But don't tell him where we are or who you're with. Nothin' he could use to find us. And make damn sure he's not with the FBI or Austin PD before you say anything they could use against either of us."

I stare at the screen for a full minute before I find the courage to dial.

"Hello?" Nelson's voice carries a hint of confusion. Not surprising since I'm sure there's no name associated with this phone number.

"It's Emi. Are you alone?" I reach for Jasper's hand. His fingers are warm and strong, and I need his touch to keep me from spiraling.

A door shuts—I think—before Nelson clears his throat. "I am now. Are you okay? Where are you? Two detectives spent an hour grilling me this morning. They say your 'friend,' Jasper Blade, killed a man at your apartment last night!"

"That man had a gun to my head, Nelson." Saying the words out loud makes what happened hit me all over again. "Jasper saved my life. We're...somewhere safe, and we're staying put for at least another couple of days. I won't have anything new to report on Monday. Not unless the FBI arrests Fowler or suddenly decides I'm worth protecting."

"Emi, I don't give a shit about the story. But there is something new to report. Fowler is suing you—and Channel 5 News—for defamation."

"For fuck's sake. He's delusional." I push to my feet and start to pace. "Email me all the details. I'll send you an audio file you can play during the A-block on Monday."

"We'll run it. I promise. But stay safe. Please."

I rub my hand over my heart to ease the ache deep in my chest. "I should go. But...is Kyle okay? No one's gone after him or his family?"

"Kyle's fine. He misses working with you, but he's killing it on midday, and his wife is happy to have him home for dinner every night. Fowler's only focused on you."

Jasper

Spending the day with Emi was better than I could have imagined. I even liked the kale. Kind of like spinach with more backbone.

If only the conversation with her news director had gone better. She swore a blue streak for almost five full minutes after reading the lawsuit Fowler hit her and Channel 5 with.

It took her half an hour to calm down and stop pacing after that.

The sun is arcing toward the horizon. I don't want to leave Emi's side, but I need to walk the perimeter before dark. Check the fence line, verify the motion sensors are all working, set a handful of tripwires...

Emi's wrapped in a blanket on the couch with her tablet balanced on her thighs, but when I pull on my coat, she frowns. "You're not going anywhere, are you?"

"Gotta check the gas level in the generator and make sure no one's been snoopin' around the fence line. I won't be long."

"Can I come with you?" Emi sets the tablet on the coffee table and rolls her head from side to side. "I haven't been outside all day."

"All right. But you stay close. I can't protect you if I can't see you."

I bundle her up in one of AJ's jackets, then grab my SIG from the bedside table and clip the holster to my belt.

Emi eyes the gun. "I don't suppose you have another one of those, do you?"

"Come again?"

"I was born in Texas, Jasper. I know how to shoot."

Fuck. This woman gets hotter every minute. I return to the safe and find a Glock 19 for her. In under ten seconds, she's dropped the mag and checked the chamber.

"I've shot one of these before," she says, flipping the safety on, then slamming the magazine back into place. "Stop looking at me like that, Jasper."

"Like what?" As soon as she has the gun secured in the little hip holster, I slide my hand around her waist. "Like you're an amazing woman and I'd do near anythin' for the chance to see where this goes?"

Her cheeks flush in the late afternoon sun coming through the front window.

"You...uh...you can keep on with that look."

"Oh, really?" Dipping my head, I plant a kiss to the tip of her nose. "Is that a yes?"

"I didn't hear a question," she teases.

Drawing back enough to meet her gaze, I slide my left leg between her thighs. "Will you consider bein' with me when this is all over? Long term?"

"Why, Jasper Blade, I don't know what to say." She grins, light dancing in her eyes.

"Say yes."

I punctuate the words by scoring my teeth along the shell of her ear, and she shudders in my arms.

"Yes. Absolutely. As long as you promise to do that again," she says, her voice not entirely steady.

"Oh, I can *definitely* promise you that, sweetheart. That and a whole lot more."

CHAPTER EIGHTEEN

Emi

IF IT WEREN'T for the threat hanging over our heads, this would have been the perfect day. The perfect night too.

Jasper built a fire in the wood stove, and we're cuddling under blankets on the couch while getting to know one another.

Before sunset, we walked around the whole property. This time of year, there aren't many others up at the lake. The temperature was falling fast by the time we got back to the cabin. It might even snow tonight.

With the drapes drawn, hiding us from the rest of the world, we've talked about everything and nothing. Childhood dreams. Adult realities.

I'm full of perfectly cooked steak and roasted vegetables—the last of my grocery order—and Jasper even opened a bottle of wine from a surprisingly well-stocked cellar. He only had half a glass, but I'm on my second, and the slight buzz is making me a bit brazen.

"Tell me about these," I say as I stroke my fingers gently over his right cheek. The scars are small. I'd barely noticed them before, but up close, with the firelight dancing along his skin, they're impossible to miss.

"You covered the explosion." Jasper sits up a little straighter, and the blanket falls away. "Not much more to tell. Lost most of my peripheral vision in that eye."

My heart squeezes at the pain in his voice. "I reported on the *investigation*. But DPS media relations wouldn't tell me anything about your injuries. Just that you were in serious condition. You kicked me out of your hospital room before I could ask in person." I cover his hand with mine and squeeze his fingers. He's been rubbing his right leg on and off all night.

"Dislocated shoulder. Torn rotator cuff. Broken collarbone. They had to replace my hip and put three pins in my femur. Hurts like a sombitch every damn day, but at least I can still walk. Even run if I have to. But I'll pay for it."

Raking his hand through his hair, he stares at the flames dancing in the wood stove. "About what I said earlier...? I ain't a good bet long term."

I sit up and grab his shoulders to force him to look at me. "Now listen here, Jasper. You can't *un-ask* me out on a date."

"Emi." There's an edge to his voice now that wasn't there a moment ago. His eyes harden. "I don't have a job. Bein' a Ranger? I was *good* at that. Now, I'm the super at my apartment building. I fix shit and collect the rent. You need someone...better."

"That's horse shit, and you know it." My accent is back, and I don't care one bit. "I'm a forty-year-old woman in a business that *abhors* wrinkles. In another five or six years, there won't be a place for me on the nightly news. Not unless I get damn lucky or find a niche market that doesn't care when my laugh lines get deep enough you could mine for gold in them. Your job is just that... your *job*."

"I don't know who I am without that star on my shirt!" he snaps.

"I do." I trail my fingers along his jaw. "You're the guy who saved my kale. Who refused to let me take a rideshare home from the hospital. Who slept on my floor to make sure I was okay. Who gave me the last piece of cornbread. I like that guy. A lot. I want to date him. Maybe clear out a drawer for him. Or... more."

Jasper pulls me into his arms. His kiss is all consuming, setting me on fire until I can't think straight.

I need him naked. Right now.

"Bedroom." I push to my feet, take his hand, and drag him down the hall. But when he eases me down to the blankets, pain creases lines around his eyes.

I panic until I see how tight the front of his jeans are.

"Come here." Pushing up on an elbow, I reach for his belt buckle. "I want you naked."

"Are you sure?"

"Some reason I shouldn't be?" I cup his cheek, his beard almost soft under my palm. "I was sure last night. Before... everything."

He strips off his flannel shirt, and son of a biscuit. His arms are seriously cut, and I can see the evidence of what used to be a six pack—or more—though the ridges have gone soft.

Sitting on the bed with his back to me, he sighs. "After I retired —after I was *forced* to retire—well, I spent too many nights just sittin' in my recliner with a bottle—or three—of Shiner rather than takin' care of myself. And the explosion did a lot of damage."

"Jasper Blade. If you think I'm that shallow—"

"No!" The word escapes on a snarl. Strong arms band around me, pulling me into his lap so I can tuck my head under his chin. "I ain't been with anyone in three years, Emi. What I feel for you... I can't explain it."

"Then stop talking, and *show* me."

Sliding my hands between us, I find his belt and loosen the buckle.

"If you think I give two shits how many abs you have...well, you're smarter than that, Jasper. Kiss me, and let me prove how very much I do *not* care. You hear?"

With a little twist of my hips, I grind myself against his arousal.

"Emi...fuuuuuuck," he groans. "You keep doin' that, I'm gonna come before I even get you naked."

"Well, that's no fun." I wriggle off his lap and strip off my sweater. My nipples pebble under my bra. "Your move."

He gets to his feet. The light from the bedside lamp hits his torso. Deep scars traverse his right shoulder. Half a dozen of them, at least. Burns wrap around his obliques and disappear into his jeans.

I press my lips to the deepest scar along his collarbone, and he shudders.

With each kiss, Jasper relaxes a bit more. At least until I score my teeth over one of his nipples. He hisses out a breath, followed by a whispered, "Goddamn, Emi."

Swirling my tongue over the tight nub, I relish in his every reaction. In the hint of salt on his skin. His scent. The way his fingers slide into my hair and tighten around the strands.

"Off," he grunts and tugs at my leggings. "I need to see you."

I only pause my ministrations long enough for him to strip off my clothes—and shed his own pants.

Holy hell. Dark blue boxer briefs strain over his erection. He climbs onto the bed, straddling me. "What do you like, sweetheart?"

With a grin, I wrap my arms around his neck and pull his lips to mine. "To be on top."

Jasper

Damn. Emi swivels her hips, and all the blood in my body heads south. I can't remember the last time I was *this* turned on.

"You'll get your chance," I say as I kiss along her jaw. "But not until I've tasted you. All of you."

Her pretty manicured nails rake down my back. The sensation lands somewhere between pleasure and pain. Fuck me. There ain't a damn thing I won't do for this woman. Closing my teeth over the shell of her ear, I bite down hard enough for her to shiver.

"You like that?" With one more tug, I turn my focus to her neck. Her pulse throbs under my lips, and my mouth waters from the slight hint of salt on her skin.

"God...yes. More." Her voice takes on a low, raspy tone, and it might be the sexiest fucking thing I've ever heard.

My palm molds to one full breast, and her nipple rises to meet my thumb. She shudders under me, eyes half-lidded. I swirl my tongue around her other tight nub, then suck it between my teeth.

She clutches my shoulders hard enough, I'll have bruises in the morning, but I don't care. The arch of her back and the moan spilling from her parted lips are worth it.

I bite and suck and kiss until her skin starts to glisten. The scent of her arousal fills the room. Sliding down her body, I press my lips to a long, curved scar above her mound.

"Jasper..." The uncertainty in her voice is too much for me. "Don't look at—"

I lift my gaze to hers. "What was it you said a bit ago? 'If you think I'm that shallow'?" To prove my point, I take her hand and press it to the bulge in my boxer briefs.

For several seconds, we're frozen in time. How can she think there's a single damn thing about her that isn't beautiful? That isn't sexy as hell?

And then it hits me.

The same way I can call myself a washed-up, broken-down has been.

"I wish this had never happened." I punctuate my words with half a dozen kisses from one end of the scar to the other. "But only because I know you'd change it if you could. Not because it makes you anythin' less than fucking perfect."

A tear slips from the corner of her eye. "I don't deserve you, Jasper," she whispers.

"No, sweetheart. I'm the one who doesn't deserve you."

Emi

Cupping the back of Jasper's neck, I pull his lips to mine. I *know* the miscarriage, the infection, and the resulting surgery weren't my fault. But the last man I slept with—more than five years ago— took one look at my naked body and turned off the light before he went down on me.

Jasper didn't just look at my scar. He *kissed* it. And I can feel how hard he is.

My own arousal slicks my thighs. My breasts ache, heavy with need. The rasp of his chest hair against my nipples is almost too much. Slowly, I swivel my hips under him. A growl rumbles through him, deep and possessive, while his tongue does delicious things to my mouth.

"No fair," he manages when we come up for air. "I had a plan, and you're messin' with it."

"A plan, huh?" His hair slips through my fingers as he slides between my thighs. "What about *my* plan? The one where I'm on top?"

"We'll get there." With a wicked grin, he presses his nose to my entrance and inhales, deeply. "Hold on to somethin'."

The first flick of his tongue to my clit has me seeing stars. Desperate, I claw at the sheets, dig my heels against the mattress, and arch my back.

Jasper laps, sucks, and bites like I'm a banquet laid out for him and him alone. This isn't sex. This is...more. So much more. "Oh... God. Yes. Right...there..."

His laugh against my lower lips almost pushes me over the edge. But then he pinches my inner thigh. "Not yet, Emmylou. I'm just getting started."

Time and time again, my core tightens, my entire body starts to catch fire, but he stops to kiss me, to play with my nipples, or to tell me how beautiful I am.

Our bodies are slick with sweat, and he's not even naked yet.

"Jasper...Blade," I gasp. "Stop teasin'...and let...me...come!"

Tangling my fingers in his hair, I hold him right where I need him to be.

Another chuckle, and his tongue takes up a punishing rhythm. I let myself feel everything. The flames licking at my core. His stubble rasping against my thighs. The finger he slips inside me.

Too much. It's all too much.

He adds a second finger, then a third, stretching me wide. I can't hold back. My release races closer and closer until I implode with a feral scream and fly over the edge into oblivion.

Jasper

I'm not sure what came over me. A man should always give more than he gets, but I think I gone broke my tongue.

Despite all the tender words we've said to one another tonight, Emi ain't mine. Not long term. I'll get a month with her. Two if I'm lucky. Then she'll go back to L.A. or New York, and I'll never see her again.

Maybe that's why I had to make this night unforgettable. Or maybe...I'm falling in love with the amazing woman in my arms.

She settles closer with a little sigh, and I start to pull the blankets over us. My dick is still standing at attention, but if I focus on baseball stats for an hour or three, I might still get some sleep tonight.

"Not so fast, handsome," Emi whispers, her fingers curling around the waistband of my boxer briefs. "It's my turn. Off with these."

Fuck me. If I thought I was hard before, I was wrong. "Yes, ma'am."

The dark blue material lands on the floor next to the bed. Emi gently pushes me onto my back and straddles me. A drop of precum beads on my tip.

She wraps her hand around the base of my shaft, leans down, and sucks my crown into her mouth.

"Fuuuuuck." My eyes roll back in my head. The tip of her tongue runs along the underside of my length. But when she hollows out her cheeks, my balls draw up tight. I'll come in seconds if she keeps this up.

"Inside you," I manage. "Now."

She draws back, and with a quiet *pop*, my dick slips free. "On one condition."

"God, Emi. Are you trying to kill me?"

Her sweet smile brings such light to her eyes, I don't care what her answer is. I could die a happy man right now.

Guiding me to her entrance, she eases herself down until her velvet heat surrounds me. "I want you very much alive, Jasper. And tomorrow, you're going to come down my throat."

Emi plants her hands on my chest and starts to roll her hips. She's so damn tight, I don't dare move. Hell, I'm not sure I can without shooting my load immediately.

But after a minute, she picks up the pace. I reach between us and find her clit, circling it slowly with one finger.

"Oh, God. Yes. Right there," she moans.

I want this to last, but my body has other ideas. "Kiss me. Now."

As she claims my mouth, the release I've been dreaming of for a solid week barrels through me. Her inner walls clench, and she tumbles over the edge after me.

WITH EMI'S hair fanning across my shoulder and her leg draped over mine, I might be the happiest I've ever been. Under the blankets, I trail my fingers up and down her spine. Her eyes are closed, and she hasn't moved since I turned off the light a few minutes ago.

Sleep is about to steal me away, but I press a kiss to the top of her head. Before I can stop myself, I whisper, "I'm falling in love with you, Emmylou Marsh."

Did I imagine her breath hitching? Or did she hear me? Fuck.

Why didn't I keep my damn mouth shut? It's too soon for promises of forever. But somewhere between my first taste and her last sigh, my heart decided it didn't care that our lives were headed in two different directions.

I'm damn close to loving Emi, and when the sun comes up, I'm gonna tell her.

CHAPTER NINETEEN

Emi

SOMETHING'S BEEPING. Jasper groans, and his arm tightens around my waist. But a second later, he tears the sheets from my naked body and grabs my hands.

"That's the perimeter alarm," he hisses. "Get dressed. Right now."

He throws my leggings at me, rolls out of bed, and tugs on his jeans. By the time I've found my shoes in the darkened room, he's staring at a screen on the back wall of the closet. Two red dots flash in one corner of the display.

"Fuckers cut the power, but the generator kicked in. They're comin' from the northwest." Jasper clips a holster to his waistband, then grabs his gun and two spare magazines from the nightstand.

"Give me the Glock." I hold out my hand. In the dim light coming from the closet, his expression hardens. "I know you're fixin' to tell me to stay here. But I'm safer if I have a gun."

The two red dots are getting closer. With a low rumble that's practically a growl, Jasper presses the Glock into my hand. "I only have one extra mag for this. You're goin' straight to the basement.

It's practically a safe room. One way in, one way out. Anyone comes for you there, you'll see 'em long before they see you. Start shooting and don't stop until they're dead."

Jasper leads me through the darkened house to the mudroom. Behind a coat rack there's a door I hadn't noticed earlier that leads to a set of stairs. A single light glows brightly halfway down. "Lock the deadbolt. Don't open it for anyone but me, you hear?"

"Jasper..." Pleading roughens my tone. I don't want him to go. "Wouldn't it be safer to stay together? I won't hide while you risk your life—"

He wraps his arm around my shoulders and pulls me in for a swift, hard kiss. "Yes, you will. These fuckers are pros, Emi. I can't be worryin' about you and have any hope of stoppin' them."

The desperation in his voice is too much for me. "Okay. Just... be careful."

"Shoot anyone coming down the stairs, Emi. *Anyone*. I..." He shakes his head, and the fear in his eyes almost sends me over the edge. "I'll keep you safe. Until my last breath."

He steps back and shuts the door with a quiet *click*.

Shit. My fingers slip off the deadbolt twice before I manage to lock it. I'm alone. Terrified. With a loaded gun and a spare magazine tucked in my waistband.

Yet, I'm practically untouchable compared to Jasper. He's going after those two men alone. In the dark. He was a Ranger. A State Trooper before that.

"I'm falling in love with you, Emmylou Marsh."

God, why did I pretend to be asleep when he said those sweet words to me? I wanted to say them back. I *should* have said them back. What if I don't get another chance?

Stop. Jasper won't die tonight. He knows the property, he's armed, and he has a plan. At least...I hope he has a plan.

At the bottom of the stairs, I gape at the cellar. It's at least half the size of the cabin. Shelves line the walls, full of canned goods, bottled water, half a dozen first aid kits, and blankets. There's even a ham radio down here. I wish I had any idea how to work it. Maybe I could get help. But...who would I call?

AJ is the only person Jasper trusts, and I have no idea how to get in touch with him. Even if there's a burner phone on one of these shelves, I don't have AJ's number.

Finding a spot in the corner with a clear view of the stairs, I crouch down, chamber a round in the pistol, and pray.

Jasper

The frigid night air stings my cheeks. Keeping low, I creep away from the only place I want to be—at Emi's side. The moon is close to full, giving me enough light to see a couple hundred yards, and I pick my way toward the fence line.

They were smart. The northwest corner of the property has the heaviest brush cover.

For what feels like an hour, but is probably only five minutes, I don't hear anything or anyone. Until a twig snaps behind me.

I spin around, drop to one knee, and raise the gun. Two shadows in my periphery. But one moves off to the right, and I lose him in my blind spot.

The first bullet hits the guy on the left. He goes down—hard. A dull *pop* comes from behind me. Bark explodes inches away. A shard slices my cheek.

Fuck me. There's a third man.

Who am I kidding? There could be an entire *army* surrounding the cabin right now.

Another shot grazes my bicep. I tuck and roll, coming up and firing twice. No telltale grunts. No falling bodies.

Focus!

My arm burns. Thank God it's only a scrape. Dropping to my belly, I hold my breath and listen.

A slight rustle to my left. Another twig snapping a few yards in front of me.

"Give it up, Blade. If you put down your gun, we'll make it quick. Painless, even," a man shouts.

Big mistake, shit for brains. Now I know where you are.

My boots find soft, muddy soil. Perfect for muffling my steps. The clouds are closing in, and the first snowflakes swirl in the air.

We're too close to the cabin. Too close to one of these assholes making it inside to Emi.

Someone stifles a curse, and I take aim. The moonlight is almost gone, but I can see the vague outline of his shoulder against one of the tall trees.

Two shots. One to the head, the other to the chest. He falls with only a soft exhale.

But then the cabin door closes with a bang. Fuck.

I'm too far away. I won't make it to the porch without catching a bullet. I have to try, though. Emi might be good with a gun, but these guys are pros. How many can she handle before she's out of ammo?

I take off at a dead run. Only steps from the porch, a solid weight slams into my right side. The ground rushes up to meet me, driving the air from my lungs.

A punch catches me in the jaw. I swing my arm toward my attacker, slamming the barrel of the gun against his cheek.

Blood spurts from his nose. He loses his own weapon. But he's too close. I can't get a shot off.

He knees me in the nuts. Stars burst in my vision. Gloved fingers wrap around my throat and squeeze.

The body's first instinct when deprived of air is to do whatever it takes to breathe. My limbs jerk of their own accord. I claw at the man's wrist, but he only tightens his hold.

Desperation lends me strength I shouldn't have. I slam my fist into his gut. His grip loosens slightly.

A single, raspy breath is all I get before he doubles down. It's enough.

My thumb finds his left eye. His scream is music to my ears. Bringing my other arm up sharply, I catch him in the wrist to break his hold.

"How many?" I hiss and jam the gun under his chin. If I didn't need to know, I'd end him in a heartbeat.

"Fuck. You."

Grabbing his jaw, I lean closer. "Wanna try that again? Or would you rather eat a bullet?"

"Do it. You're dead anyway."

Before I can say another word, shots come from the cabin.

Fuck. Emi!

This shitbag ain't worth my time. The bullet tears through his skull, and his body goes slack.

My hip screams at me with every step, but I ignore the pain. I have to get to Emi.

Emi

Footsteps thud over my head. There were only two red dots on the security screen, but it sounds like there are at least three people upstairs. Maybe more.

The knob rattles. Someone shouts, but the words are too muffled to make out.

Do they know I'm down here?

Wood splinters above me. They're trying to break in! Oh, God. Where's Jasper?

The door slams open, and I adjust my grip on the gun.

A man creeps slowly down the stairs. Black boots stained with mud. Black pants. Knees. Thighs. Belt. Two more steps, and I fire.

My first shot goes wide. The second and third hit him in the leg and the gut. He collapses, falling down the last few steps to the concrete floor.

Blood spreads out in a pool around him.

Another man shouts, "She's down here!"

Heavy steps race from another part of the cabin. I think there might be two more of them. I have enough bullets. I think.

I'd give anything to know where Jasper is. If three of them got inside...

Swallowing my sob, I focus on the stairs. He's okay. He has to be.

It's so quiet. Why haven't they come down already? One of the stairs creaks. I take aim, though my hands are shaking so badly, how am I supposed to hit anything?

Something hard bounces down the steps and rolls into the center of the room. I stare at the metal cylinder, confused, until a deafening *boom* fills the basement and light sears my eyes.

My ass hits the floor. I can't see. Can't hear. Can't think. My hands are glued to my ears. Where's the gun? I don't remember dropping it...

Rough hands grab my arms and haul me to my feet. Acrid smoke burns my nose. I try to pull away, but someone backhands me. The pain is like nothing I've ever felt. My entire face throbs with each beat of my heart.

"Where is it?" a voice snarls close to my ear.

"Wh-what?" Tears brim in my eyes. Shadows loom over me as my vision starts to clear.

"The recording, bitch!" The thug shakes me, hard. "Of Trowing's confession. You sent a copy to the FBI. Where's the original?"

That's what they want?

"Nowhere...you'll ever...find it," I manage. "Let me go!"

The second man slams his fist into my jaw. Blood fills my mouth, dribbling down my chin from my split lip.

"You're gonna regret fucking with us," he grits out. "Once we're back in Austin, we'll break every bone in your body one by one until you beg us to kill you."

I'm so dizzy. *Blinking* hurts. Where's Jasper? I need Jasper.

My arms are pinned behind my back, and something hard bites into my wrists.

"Noooo..." I can't let them take me. Thrashing with everything I have, I manage to get free for all of two seconds before they slam me into the nearest wall.

My bicep stings, and within seconds, my entire body starts to tingle. A gloved hand waves a syringe in front of my face. "Say goodnight, bitch."

They drag me up the stairs, one man gripping each arm as I struggle and scream for Jasper. My legs are so heavy. Like I'm stumbling through the deep end of the pool.

The walls pulse and spin. Dark spots float all around me. "Guillermo's bringing the car up now. Get her into the trunk. I'll take care of that Ranger asshole."

Jasper. He's still alive. I need to tell him...I think...I love him.

One of the men drops my arm, and the other spins me around to face him. I slam my knee into his groin. He yelps, but I wasn't strong enough. He doesn't let go.

Tears stream down my cheeks as he throws me over his shoulder. It's too hard to keep my eyes open now. I don't even try.

Cold air hits the back of my neck.

Outside. No. Can't.

"Let. Her. Go," Jasper shouts.

His voice gives me a burst of strength. I kick my legs and twist. Falling. Pain. Then...nothing.

Jasper

I unload six shots into the first asshole's chest. He doesn't make a sound as he collapses into a heap. Emi lies on her back, unmoving.

The second fucker shoots at me from inside the cabin. I dive in front of the black car idling in the driveway.

The guy in the driver's seat pulls a gun from a shoulder holster, but I put a bullet between his eyes before he can aim.

I have to get to Emi before the second shitstain does. But he's got a fuckton more firepower. A hail of gunfire hits the car, each shot plinking off the metal closer and closer to me.

The bullets stop, and I peer over the hood. No line of sight. The solid oak door opens another few inches. A hand snakes toward Emi's ankle.

Not today, fucker. Not today.

My shot blows off his pinky finger.

His strangled moan is sweet relief. And all the distraction I need.

I take all four stairs at once, jump over Emi, and hit the door. My boot lands in a pool of blood. Off balance, I go down, my bad knee slamming into the hardwood. Pain races up my leg all the way to my hip.

The fucker knocks me sideways against the door jam. My shoulder pops. A punch snaps my head back. A second catches me in the temple.

"Jas! Down!"

I dive for the floor. A deafening blast rocks the walls of the cabin. Blood sprays the back of my neck. I don't wait for the guy to hit the ground. I can't. I have to get to Emi.

AJ and I reach her at the same time. Thank God my brother knows better than to get in my way.

Gathering her in my arms, I smooth her hair away from her face. "Open your eyes, sweetheart. Please."

She's too still. But she's breathing. Slow and steady. Her cheek is bright red and hot to the touch. Blood stains her lips.

"EMS is on the way," AJ says. He takes a knee, pulls a switchblade from his pocket, and snaps the zip tie around her wrists. "How bad are you hurt?"

"Emi's all that matters. Get the first aid kit from the kitchen. I need the smelling salts."

It isn't until my brother returns that I stop to wonder why the fuck he's here.

"How did you know we were in danger?"

He rummages around in the metal box until he finds the small paper ampules of ammonia. "I've been callin' you for hours, Jas. The two FBI fuckers Emi talked to the other day were on the take. Fowler paid each of them twenty-five grand on Tuesday, and another twenty yesterday."

"Shit." I break one of the ampules and hold it under Emi's nose.

She jerks, her eyelids fluttering.

"Sweetheart, breathe for me. You're gonna be okay."

"Jasper?" Her voice is so weak and raspy, I have to strain to hear it. "Is it over?"

"It's over, Emi. I promise."

EPILOGUE

Jasper

I WATCH Emi sleep from the doorway. AJ found a syringe on the floor of the cellar and a vial of ketamine in one of the dead asshole's pockets. The sedative shouldn't have any lasting effects, thank fuck.

She refused to go to the hospital. The EMTs were livid, and AJ argued with me for a full ten minutes before I told him to shut up and let me take care of her.

Her cheek is several shades of purple. She'll be sore for days, but the bone isn't broken, and she's safe. At least for now.

AJ paces the living room, cursing every time he finds another bullet casing or drop of blood. "It's my fault, Jas. I told Van you were safe at our family cabin. I didn't know he was dirty. I swear to you. The minute the call came in—"

"You saved Emi's life, AJ. We're square."

He runs a hand through his hair, a sure sign he's pissed at himself. The man *hates* messing up his hair. "We're not. I almost got you both killed! If I hadn't called in a favor and gotten one of the best hackers in the world on the case—"

"Aaron. Don't."

He stops in his tracks and meets my gaze. Shit. It's like looking in a fuckin' mirror. Except for the pain in his eyes.

"You couldn't have known. And since you saved my ass, I think you can stop kicking yourself for five goddamn minutes."

"Don't you understand?" he shouts. "This is what I do. I fuck up, and people die."

He stalks out the front door, slamming it behind him.

Emi startles awake with a tiny whimper. I limp over to the bed and sink down next to her. "Easy, sweetheart. You're safe. We're safe."

She lets me pull her into my arms and rests her head against my chest. "What was AJ yelling about? He 'fucks up and people die'?"

My fingers tangle in her silky locks. I can't stop touching her. If I weren't so worried about her, I'd tell her how much I love her right fucking now.

"The weekend Grace disappeared, she and AJ were supposed to come up here for a long weekend. But he was gunnin' for captain at the time, and when our commander needed someone to take an overtime shift, he volunteered. Grace went out for a run that Saturday and never came home."

"Oh, God." She settles closer to me with a sigh. "He blames himself."

I stare at the front door. "He hasn't taken an easy breath in two years. Not sure he ever will again."

We sit in silence for a few minutes. I can't stop seeing her unconscious on the porch. I could have lost her. And then where would I be?

"Jasper?" Emi tightens her fingers on my flannel shirt. "I know what they were after. But it doesn't make any sense."

I tip her chin up to meet her tired gaze. "Tell me."

"I recorded my conversations with the building inspector. Alan Trowing? *That's* what they wanted tonight. The originals. But why? Even if the cartel destroyed them, the FBI still has their copy."

"Because Van and Spooner were on Fowler's payroll. That's how those assholes found us. They probably deleted the copy five minutes after you turned it over." I rub circles over her back. "Where's the original?"

"My tablet." Her words are starting to slur. "And...in the cloud. Backups of the backups."

"Good. Try to sleep a while now. I gotta find AJ. He'll have a plan for what happens next."

Easing her down, I brush my lips to the tip of her nose. There isn't another square inch of her face unmarked from the past few days.

"Wait." Emi wraps her fingers around my wrist. "Earlier...you said you were falling in love with me. I pretended to be asleep. I... shouldn't have done that."

"It's okay, sweetheart. We went from zero to somethin' fast as greased lightning. I should have kept my fool mouth shut. When this all blows over...if you ask...I'll walk away."

One corner of her mouth twitches. "You better not turn tail on me, Jasper. I'm tryin' to say 'I'm falling for you too.'"

I STAND BEHIND the cameras in the Channel 5 studio. A skeleton crew—along with Emi's news director, Nelson, came in on a Sunday afternoon so she could tape tonight's final update to the Eugene Fowler story. AJ, Parker, and three other Rangers I don't know are stationed at the doors. We'll be far away from here by the time this goes on the air.

Emi sits at the anchor desk and reads the final paragraph from the teleprompter.

"I can now report that five of the eight members of Consolidated Investment Group's Board of Directors, along with several men linked to the Cordova Cartel are in custody. Eugene Fowler is facing multiple felony charges, including conspiracy to commit murder. Construction on the Empress Hotel and Conference

Center has stopped for the foreseeable future, but the owner of the Austin Stars has vowed to personally finance the new community center. Plans are being drawn up now, and the center should open by the first of the year. For Channel 5 News, this is Emmylou Marsh, reporting."

The cameraman offers a thumbs up, and the red *Recording* light goes dark.

"That's a wrap," Nelson says. "Great job, Emi."

I limp over to her, slide my arm around her waist, and help her to her feet. "You ready to get the hell outta here?"

"God, yes. I need to sleep for a week." She leans against me, her head on my shoulder. "And maybe go more than twenty-four hours without someone trying to kill me."

"Call me in a few days," Nelson says. "Let me know when—or if—you think you can come back. Or which one of the networks steals you away."

Emi links her arm with mine and smiles. "National news isn't my end game anymore, Nelson. I'm afraid you're stuck with me."

The guy's jaw drops, and with a chuckle, I urge Emi toward the back door of the studio. AJ's waiting for us.

"What about me?" I ask as we step into the afternoon sun. "Am I stuck with you, too?"

Emi laughs. "I think you might be. Turns out, I'm in love with you, Jasper."

"If you two are done making googly eyes at each other, can we go?" AJ drawls, leaning against the SUV with his arms crossed. "A friend of a friend set the two of you up at the Five Points Austin for the next week. It'll give the Feds time to make sure the corruption didn't go any higher than Van and Spooner."

"The Five Points? When did the Rangers start springing for a hotel *that* nice?" I ask.

He snorts. "Never. The 'friend of a friend' took care of it. Don't ask questions. I won't answer them."

Well, at least my brother's back to his usual grumpy self. For a few minutes at the cabin, I thought maybe, we'd built some sort of bridge between us. But it's gone now.

I bring Emi's hand to my lips. "I love you, Emmylou Marsh. When this is all over, move in with me? Or move...somewhere with me? Or let me move in with you?"

She tries to smile, but winces as her fingers fly to her swollen lip. "I ruined the moment." The words are a little awkward and muffled behind her hand. "Ask me again tomorrow?"

It takes a beat before I understand. "Ask you again, huh? So you can say 'yes' properly?"

Her eyes narrow. "I'm usually the one with the trick questions."

"Take the day off, sweetheart. I think you've earned it." Leaning over as far as the seatbelt will let me, I cup the back of her neck and carefully seal my lips to hers.

We're both breathless when she pulls back to whisper in my ear. "Will you ask me again tomorrow, Jasper?"

"Yes, ma'am. I sure will."

***

THANK you for reading Blade's Edge! This is the first book in the L.A.S.T. Defense series. There are currently four books planned for the series. Each book is a standalone, but I love bringing back characters for supporting roles later on.

AJ's book is Stone's Throw, and you can grab it now!

All of my protector romantic suspense novels cross over with one another. I'd love it if you'd check out Breaking His Code, the first book in my award-winning Away From Keyboard series. It's free on my website in both eBook and audio.

Both Jasper and AJ also show up in Rogue Survivor. Do you like single-mom-of-a-teenager finds love at the gym with a hunky-but-broken-former-FBI agent protector books? Then you will absolutely love Rogue Survivor.

If you liked this book, I hope you'll consider signing up for my mailing list. You'll get TWO free romantic suspense short stories that aren't available anywhere else! Plus behind the scenes information about past and future books, new release news, and more!

You can also join my Facebook group, **Patricia's Unstoppable Forces**. It's a great, supportive place for all things beautifully broken.

Love, Patricia

ABOUT THE AUTHOR

Patricia D. Eddy is a USA Today bestselling author who writes romance for the beautifully broken. Fueled by coffee, wine, and *Doctor Who* episodes on repeat, she brings damaged heroes and heroines together to find their happy ever afters in many different worlds. From military to paranormal to BDSM, her characters are unstoppable forces colliding with such heat, sparks always fly.

Patricia makes her home in Seattle with her husband and very spoiled cats, and when she's not writing, she loves working on home improvement projects, especially if they involve power tools.

Her award-winning *Away From Keyboard* series will always be her first love, because that's where she realized the characters in her head were telling their own stories—and she was just writing them down.

facebook.com/patriciadeddyauthor

x.com/patriciadeddy

instagram.com/patriciadeddy

bookbub.com/profile/patricia-d-eddy

tiktok.com/@patriciadeddyauthor

ALSO BY PATRICIA D. EDDY

Away From Keyboard

Dive into a steamy mix of geekery and military prowess with the men and women of Hidden Agenda and Second Sight.

Breaking His Code

In Her Sights

On His Six

Second Sight

By Lethal Force

Fighting For Valor

Finding Their Forevers (a holiday short story)

Call Sign: Redemption

Braving His Past

Protecting His Target

Defending His Hope

Trusting His Instincts

Saving Their Forever (an Away From Keyboard novella)

Guarding His Heart

Gone Rogue (an Away From Keyboard spinoff series)

Rogue Protector

Rogue Officer

Rogue Survivor

Rogue Defender

Rogue Operator

Rogue Mission

Dark PNR

These novellas will take you into the darker side of the paranormal with vampires, witches, angels, demons, and more.

Forever Kept

Immortal Hunter

Wicked Omens

Storm of Sin

Gabriel's Gambit

Elemental Shifter

Pick up the COMPLETE Elemental Shifter series for thrilling tales of werewolves and magic.

A Shift in the Water

A Shift in the Air

A Shift in the Earth

A Shift in Fire

By the Fates

Check out the COMPLETE By the Fates series if you love dark and steamy tales of witches, devils, and an epic battle between good and evil.

By the Fates, Freed

Destined: A By the Fates Story

By the Fates, Fought

By the Fates, Fulfilled

In Blood

If you love hot Italian vampires and and a human who can hold her own against beings far stronger, then the In Blood series is for you.

Secrets in Blood

Revelations in Blood

Holidays and Heroes

Beauty isn't only skin deep and not all scars heal. Come swoon over sexy vets and the men and women who love them.

Mistletoe and Mochas

Love and Libations

Targets and True Love

Restrained

Do you like to be tied up? Or read about characters who do? Enjoy a fresh COMPLETE BDSM series that will leave you begging for more.

In His Silks

Christmas Silks

All Tied Up For New Year's

In His Collar